A Vow of Devotion

A Vow of Devotion

VERONICA BLACK

St. Martin's Press
New York
❧

Library of Congress Cataloging-in-Publication Data

Black, Veronica.
A vow of devotion / Veronica Black.
p.   cm.
ISBN 0-312-13206-9
1. Joan, Sister (Fictitious character)—Fiction.   2. Women
detectives—England—Cornwall (County)—Fiction.   3. Nuns—
England—Cornwall (County)—Fiction.   4. Cornwall (England :
County)—Fiction.   I. Title.
PR6052.L335V683   1995
823'.914—dc20   95-16054   CIP

First published in Great Britain by Robert Hale Limited

First U.S. Edition: July 1995
10 9 8 7 6 5 4 3 2 1

A Vow of Devotion

One

It was a day for feeling hopeful and optimistic. Sister Joan, who seldom felt anything else, led Lilith, the convent pony, out into the cobbled yard and mounted up, secure in the knowledge that if the breeze blew up the skirt of her grey habit she was wearing jeans underneath, a special concession permitted by her prioress, Mother Dorothy, who came now to the kitchen door and looked out, gold-rimmed spectacles clamped firmly to her beaky nose, her hands folded in approved fashion within the wide sleeves of the dark purple habit which signified her position as head of this particular community of sisters of the Order of Daughters of Compassion. When her five-year term was over she would wear a purple band on the right sleeve of her grey habit to remind her of the office she had held. Rather like a sergeant's stripes, Sister Joan thought with an inward grin, composing her face as she turned dark-blue eyes towards her superior.

'Do you want me to pick up anything else for you in town?' she asked.

'I don't think so, Sister. You'll check the velvet is good quality?'

'Yes, of course, Mother. Sister Teresa is going to look beautiful, isn't she?'

'And velvet is such a sensible choice,' Mother Dorothy said briskly. 'It can be quite chilly at this time of year and one doesn't want to see a Bride of Christ shiver her way through her final vows. You'll look in on Father Malone?'

'Yes, Mother.' Sister Joan bowed her veiled head for the

swift blessing sketched upon the air and trotted beneath the arch and down the side path to the drive which curved between lawn and shrubbery to the moorland track.

In Cornwall spring often came sooner than in other parts of the country, and this spring was no exception. The turf was starred with wild flowers and there was a faint golden haze on the horizon that hinted at a fine day to come.

'Come, Lilith!' Sister Joan slapped the pony on her rump and broke into a canter. Behind her she heard a doleful whining from Alice, the year-old Alsatian bitch acquired originally as a guard dog for the isolated community. Sister Joan had taken the precaution of tying Alice up before she set out since a gambolling dog wasn't the most desirable companion for a trip into town. Her conscience was less stricken than it might have been since she knew perfectly well that Sister Perpetua would take Alice's mind off her imprisonment with a few choice titbits. The infirmarian had a soft spot for animals though she would have been unwilling to admit it, having long since cast herself in the role of a red-haired, peppery individual with no time for sentiment.

And what role do I see myself in? Sister Joan thought, checking her speed and holding Lilith to a more decorous pace.

Thirty-eight years old, having turned her back on marriage or a career as an artist nearly ten years before to enter the religious life, she mused, trying to stand outside herself mentally and take the objective viewpoint. Not, she suspected, an ideal nun though she tried hard to fit her lively and impestuous nature to the even tenor of community life. Certainly not a Living Rule, that nun whose conduct would make it possible to write out again the rules of the order should they ever be lost. There were times when she doubted if a Living Rule had ever existed in actuality.

She slowed further as a small stone building came into view. The building had once provided a school where local children could be taught before going into town to the 'big' school. She herself had been the teacher, with a small class composed of local children and a few from the Romany camp high on the moor. She had enjoyed her period of teaching until new regulations had forced the school to close. Now the stone building stood mute and locked, its windows boarded up. It was still convent property but nobody had thought of a proper use for it.

As she turned into the main street of the town she decided she would call first on Father Malone. Sister Jerome who had kept house for him and the curate, Father Stephens, since the former's return from his sabbatical abroad, couldn't be said to be an amiable woman but she made splendid coffee.

Sister Joan dismounted, leading Lilith down the side alley which bisected the streets and provided a short cut to the church and presbytery, both modest structures since in this predominantly Protestant corner of England the Catholic Church still existed more or less on sufferance and trod cautiously to avoid offence.

As she tied Lilith to the garden gate the front door opened and Father Malone came out, beaming in his usual welcoming fashion.

'Sister Joan, *bonjour* as they say! All's well?'

'All's well, Father.' Sister Joan bit her lip to stifle a giggle. Father Malone had been lacing his conversation with foreign phrases ever since his return from his sabbatical five months before.

'Come in, Sister. You didn't bring the car?' He came close enough to give Lilith the lump of sugar in his hand.

'Lilith is easier on the petrol,' Sister Joan said with a grin. 'You spoil her, Father.'

'Now isn't a pony a living beast now?' he countered, dropping into his native brogue. 'Sure but it's a breathing, feeling thing and, if His Holiness is right, the owner of a soul which will open the doors to an afterlife.'

'I'm sure His Holiness *is* right,' Sister Joan said, following the priest back up the path. 'I never could imagine heaven without a few animals around.'

'The blessed St Francis would have blessed you for that,

Sister,' Father Malone approved. 'You know I helped offer mass at Assisi. I've some photographs somewhere. Or perhaps you have already seen them?'

Everybody in the convent had seen them several times. Father Malone had gone off on pilgrimage clutching missal and camera with almost equal regard for both.

'I'd love to take a look at them, Father,' she said. 'One doesn't get the chance for a proper look with everybody crowding round.'

'They're about here somewhere.' Father Malone led the way to the study, looked round vaguely and pounced on the buff folder. 'Here we are! Sit yourself down and I'll ask Sister Jerome to make us a nice cup of coffee. I've an idle half-hour this morning since Father Stephens very kindly offered to visit the old people's home.'

'That's very nice of him,' Sister Joan said diplomatically.

From what she'd heard Father Stephens, who was young, educated and ambitious, was apt to talk rather too much about the twilight of life and the gates of heaven standing open when he was with anyone over the age of sixty.

'Many of the poor souls are getting very deaf, you know,' Father Malone said, a slight twinkle in his eyes betraying that he shared her reservations. 'Ah, Sister Jerome, here you are! And with coffee already!'

'I heard Sister Joan's voice.' Sister Jerome put down the tray and nodded her head in Sister Joan's direction. 'Good morning, Sister Joan.'

'Good morning, Sister Jerome.' Answering pleasantly, receiving a frosty smile before the priests' housekeeper went plodding back to the kitchen, Sister Joan reminded herself that Sister Jerome had a sad history and was more in her element here ministering to men of the cloth than trying to live with a crowd of women.*

'Help yourself to sugar, Sister. Now let me see – this is of the façade of the cathedral. You can judge its size if you

---

* See *Vow of Penance*

realize that the figure by the portico is myself and I'm five feet seven. A friar was kind enough to take the picture for me. He took another, a close-up but it came out a mite fuzzy. I was coming to the end of that roll of film.'

Sister Joan shook her head to the sugar and the chocolate finger which marked the end of Lent and looked dutifully at the photographs, marvelling at her own ability to say something freshly complimentary about each one.

'I've the ones from Lourdes somewhere around,' Father Malone said hopefully.

'Father, once you tempt me into looking at photographs of Lourdes I'll be here all morning,' she said, laughing. 'I only came to ask you if everything's being made ready for Sister Teresa's final profession. I'm sure that it is but you know Mother Dorothy likes all her i's dotted and her t's crossed in good time.'

'Everything's going ahead very smoothly, Sister,' he assured her. 'His Lordship will be here in a month's time, staying overnight at the presbytery, of course, and there'll be a concelebrated mass up in the convent chapel. She'll be looking forward to it – Sister Teresa.'

'I'm sure she will, but of course she's still in retreat,' Sister Joan said.

After the postulancy and the novitiate intending Daughters of Compassion spent a year in virtual silence and isolation before taking their perpetual vows of poverty, chastity, obedience and compassion.

'A pity she wasn't able to make her profession last Easter,' he regretted.

'Circumstances delayed her entry into retreat as you know, Father. In a way the delay will work to our advantage, I think,' Sister Joan said, rising. 'Not being able to join fully in the celebrations at Easter with the rest of us means she starts out with a sacrifice and then, having her own ceremony after Easter, will make it a real landmark day.'

'Without having to compete with the risen Christ for the attention of the community?' Father Malone shook his grey head at her reproachfully.

'I didn't mean it quite like that, Father,' she protested.

'I'm sure you didn't. Whatever the circumstances I'm sure Sister Teresa's day will be a wonderfully happy one. You have errands to do?'

'I'm collecting the material for Sister Teresa's dress. Is it all right if I leave Lilith here? She dislikes being ridden through traffic.'

'As long as you please, Sister. The traffic will be getting worse here soon, I'm afraid.' He rose to accompany her to the door.

'Tourists so early?' Sister Joan looked at him.

'New Age Travellers,' Father Malone said, giving each word a large, doleful capital letter. 'Apparently a large group are headed this way.'

'They'll probably camp out of town on the moor,' she said.

'One hopes so.' Father Malone, who liked his fellow human beings to be in neat categories, sighed. 'It's very difficult to draw the line between freedom and licence, isn't it? We shall just have to pray that they don't cause too much damage. Give my regards to Mother Prioress and the community. Does Sister Teresa intend to continue as lay sister after her profession?'

'We're all hoping so,' Sister Joan said. 'A year of my cooking is about as much as the community can endure. Goodbye, Sister Jerome.'

From the kitchen door Sister Jerome afforded her a curt nod before returning to the sink.

The line between lay and semi-enclosed sister was in the Daughters of Compassion as fine as between the freedom and licence the priest had remarked upon, she mused, as she strode off down the main street, the ends of her short white veil fluttering in the spring breeze. Within the community the nuns remained within the confines of the enclosure, earning their living as far as was possible from their home base. Only the lay sisters went out to do the marketing and, in return for that small freedom, lived more separately than their sisters, taking their meals and recreation separately, the Marthas of the community. Sister Teresa's year-long retreat had imposed a certain loneliness on Sister Joan too. Mother Prioress had hinted that if Sister Teresa chose to continue as lay sister she herself might be considered as assistant mistress of novices. Not that she considered herself a suitable mistress of anyone but it would be nice to write home and tell her family about it. Her mother would certainly regard it as a promotion. In her letters she frequently hinted what a thrill it would be if her only daughter got elected as prioress one day.

'To which dizzy heights I am unlikely to aspire,' Sister Joan muttered and walked full tilt into a tall man walking in the opposite direction.

'Talking to yourself, Sister Joan? Times must be desperate!'

Detective Sergeant Alan Mill took a pace backwards and looked down at her, one dark eyebrow raised in amusement.

'It's probably the onset of my twilight years,' Sister Joan said. 'How are you, Detective Sergeant Mill?'

'Well enough.' He gave her a second look. 'And you, Sister? It's months since we've met.'

'I don't come into town more than once a month and then I'm usually in the car. I rode in today on Lilith.'

'Not shopping?'

'Sister Teresa makes her final profession next month and I'm here to pick up the material for her dress.'

'Dress?' His eyebrow rose again.

'Wedding dress,' she said provocatively, waiting for the scowl.

It came, reminding her of Jacob whom she seldom thought about these days except when she ran into the detective. Both were dark, lean men, Detective Sergeant Mill having the advantage in height and a chiselled profile while Jacob had borne the palm for intensity of dark eyes and quick, nervous gesture.

'You can't expect an agnostic to be very thrilled at the prospect of a healthy young woman getting herself togged up to exchange marriage vows with someone who was executed nearly two thousand years ago,' he said.

'You must allow us our eccentricities,' she said lightly, but there was a flash of concern at the back of her eyes.

Detective Sergeant Mill had never spoken so sourly of religious matters before. He and she had, at the beginning of their acquaintanceship, tacitly agreed to beg to differ. He had always shown respect towards her beliefs, and she had gleaned the impression that he was more sympathetic than otherwise to the Faith.

'Sorry, Sister,' he said quickly. 'That was rude and insensitive. The truth is that I'm not in a mood to talk about marriage today.'

He had told her once, briefly and casually in passing, that he and his wife were having problems, but she had never enquired further. Nor would she do so now. It was no business of hers how a man with whom she had been associated in his professional capacity lived in private. Before she could change the subject, however, he said, 'My wife's asked me for a divorce and I've agreed.'

'I'm truly sorry.' Her expression had darkened slightly.

Divorce was always a sad end to a relationship and in this case there were children.

'We're merely closing the book on a tale that was told quite a long time ago,' he said. 'She'll take the boys but I'll have ample access. There's nobody else involved.'

'Then couldn't you—?'

'Not unless I left the Force and I'm not prepared to do that. It's not her fault. When we first married she didn't realize – neither of us realized – the inroads the job makes into one's private time. We've lived apart for two years in fact if not in name so there won't be any difficulties.'

'Aren't there places you can go for counselling these days?' she ventured.

'We're neither of us interested,' he said.

'Then I am sorry,' she repeated gently. 'I can understand how you feel when I go on about Sister Teresa's final profession. It must seem like a medieval mockery to you.'

'I wish her happiness anyway,' he said. 'How's the dog getting on? Alice?'

'Alice is a joy and a delight,' Sister Joan said, relieved to have moved away from the personal.

'I gave her to the community as a guard dog.'

'Oh, she's that too – or will be when she's completed her training,' Sister Joan assured him. 'She's very intelligent and obedient.'

'I'll call one of these days and see how she's getting on.'

'You'll be very welcome, Detective Sergeant Mill. How are things apart from—?'

'On the work front everything's very quiet – for the moment. We've just had word that a group of new-age travellers are headed in this direction. If we all keep very quiet they might pass on by.'

'You don't approve?'

'Not much.'

'You know,' she said, smiling as the thought occurred to her, 'I suppose that Our Blessed Lord and His disciples were rather like new-age travellers in their day – a group of men with a sprinkling of women journeying about in the Holy Land, not staying quietly in their homes and minding their own business.'

'I doubt if Jesus and His friends smoked hash or claimed Social Security benefits,' Detective Sergeant Mill said dryly.

'Probably not! Will you try to move them on then?'

'I'll try to persuade them not to stay too long,' he said grimly.

'You don't mind the gypsies.'

'There's been a Romany camp up on the moor for nearly three hundred years, Sister. They earn a living of a sort; pay their fines or serve their time if they fall foul of the law, and don't interfere with the rest of us. We've a live and let live policy towards them. The other lot are different. If they give you any trouble at the convent let us know.'

'Oh, Alice will see them off,' Sister Joan said cheerfully. 'It was nice seeing you again.'

'You too, Sister. Take care now.'

He saluted her with a slight lifting of his hand and went on past her down the street. She turned to stare after him, frowning a little. From the beginning there had been an unspoken understanding between them that anything in the nature of a personal friendship was out of the question. She had helped him in a couple of cases in which she had become innocently involved and when the last report had been written they went their separate ways. That he should speak so readily of his impending divorce demonstrated his bitterness. That might indicate there was some feeling left in him for his estranged wife. She resolved to pray about it and went on briskly.

The smooth folds of velvet were a soft ivory in shade. There would be sufficient over for a heart-shaped cap from which a plain white veil would descend. Sister Teresa had chosen to carry lilies and white rosebuds. With her dark hair and brown eyes she was going to look lovely.

Paying for the material, watching the assistant parcel it up, she remembered her own dress, of white muslin with a ruffled hem, and white carnations because it had been summer and anything heavier than muslin would have swamped her small, slight frame. Her parents and both her brothers had been there, looking unfamiliar in their best go-to-church clothes, her mother's face shaded by a wide-brimmed hat so that it was impossible to see if she was shedding a few tears or not. Jacob hadn't come.

'No point in prolonging the agony,' Jacob had said, when they'd finally decided that he couldn't bring himself to marry a Gentile and she had known that she couldn't bring herself to convert to Judaism much as she respected that ancient faith.

She'd waited nearly a year before applying to the Order of the Daughters of Compassion, sent Jacob a brief note telling him of her decision, emphasizing that this was what she wanted to do with the rest of her life, but he hadn't written back and he hadn't come to see her make her final profession.

She had no idea whether or not Sister Teresa had left an ex-boyfriend behind, had ever had a boyfriend. In her early twenties, rosy and amiable with a calm, unfurrowed brow Teresa looked as if she had been preparing for the religious life since childhood.

She came out into the street again, the bulky parcel under her arm, and walked back towards the presbytery. People were doing their morning shopping, a few nodding to her pleasantly as she passed. In the years since the community had taken over the old Tarquin estate the presence of a nun or two in the town occasioned little comment.

Father Stephens, blond and urbane, was just approaching the gate as she strapped the parcel into the saddle-bag and untied Lilith.

'Good morning, Sister Joan. Are you coming in?'

'No, I'm on my way back to the convent, Father. Did you have a good visit at the old people's home?'

'Inspiring,' he said. 'Being with old people humbles one, don't you find? Such experience! Such nobility!'

'I'm sure you're right, Father,' Sister Joan said kindly.

In her opinion age didn't always confirm either experience or nobility. Bad-tempered young people simply became more so as they aged, but Father Stephens was still an idealist with no glimmerings of any sense of humour. He would probably end up as a bishop, she thought, and mounted Lilith hastily lest her twinkling eyes betray the course her thoughts were taking.

'You've heard the news, I suppose, about the new-age travellers coming?' In just such sepuchral tones might a Saxon monk have announced that Viking longships were on the horizon.

'Yes, but they're not here yet, are they?' she said aloud.

'One hopes they will go elsewhere,' he said.

'But then someone else will have the inconvenience.'

'You're right, Sister. That was a selfish thought though I fear I'm not the only one thinking it,' he said. 'Perhaps one should welcome them. Many must feel rootless, seeking their pleasure in drugs and er – other things.'

'Sex, do you mean?' Sister Joan gathered up the reins.

Father Stephens betrayed his youth by blushing bright red.

'I tried it once,' he said.

'Good Lord, Father!' She stared at him and he went, if possible, a deeper shade of scarlet as he said hastily, 'Marijuana, Sister. What they call "hash". A few of us got hold of some in school and smoked it. Well, I only had a couple of puffs before I felt sick but I feel I have some experience of "being high".'

'Indeed you have, Father. It gives you something in common with the junkies,' she said gravely.

'It gives me a slight advantage if I come into contact with them,' he agreed. 'What I just told you is confidential, of course, Sister. I'd not wish to shock Father Malone.'

Father Malone would probably be relieved and amused to learn his curate had a weakness, she thought, but answered promptly, 'Of course, Father Stephens. I'll not say a word. Good day to you.'

'God bless you, Sister.'

He signed a large cross upon the air and turned in at the gate. He already had the long sweeping step of a bishop, she thought, watching him go in with a feeling of exasperated tenderness. She didn't like to admit it but she was fond of Father Stephens because of his faults and not despite them.

Riding back up the track that crossed the moor she was conscious, as she always was, of the beauty of her surroundings. The mother house where she had done her training was in the middle of the city with traffic noises interfering with the peace of the cloister. Here there was peace and isolation, the flower-starred grass broken by an occasional patch of peat, dark against the surrounding green, the pale haze of the far hills thrown into focus by a tree standing slantways against the wind.

Dismounting at the convent gate she stood for a moment to enjoy the loveliness of the old house. Not even the 'improvements' inflicted on it by Victorian builders could entirely ruin the classical severity of walls and roof and window lintels. The great house had been built of granite, its tiled roof now worn by age to a silvery grey, its chimneys smokeless since there was heating only in the infirmary and then only in the coldest part of the winter.

'Sister Joan!' Little Sister Martha who did the gardening, lifting huge loads with an ease that belied her delicate appearance, came speeding down the drive. 'Sister, Mother Dorothy asked me to look out for you. She wants to see you in the parlour.'

'I wonder what I've done wrong now,' Sister Joan said.

'Oh, I'm sure you haven't done anything, Sister.' Sister Martha's pale face was startled. 'She seemed in an excellent humour. Shall I take Lilith back for you?'

'Thank you, Sister, and will you give Sister Katharine the velvet for Sister Teresas dress? It's in the saddle-bag.'

'White velvet. How elegant that will look! I had silk with tiny white and gold flowers embroidered all over it,' Sister Martha said with pleasurable recollection replacing the start-led look. 'My godmother bought the material for me. Come along, Lilith.'

She took the reins and set off up the drive, leaving Sister Joan to follow more pensively.

Despite Sister Martha's reassurances it was seldom that Mother Dorothy invited one into the parlour for a happy little chat. On the other hand Sister Joan couldn't bring to mind any recent infractions of the rule that called for scolding.

She went in through the front door, leaving Sister Martha to lead the pony round to the back.

The main hall with its sweeping staircase was polished as usual to the acme of shining slipperiness. To the left and right arched doorways led respectively to the antechamber with the prioress's parlour beyond and into the chapel wing where a narrow corridor led past the visitors' parlour with its dividing grille into the long chapel with its tiny sacristy leading off it. There were no decorations but the height of the ceiling with its swags of white plaster grapes, the intricate carving of the balustrade made gilding the lily unnecessary.

She straightened her veil, pushed back an errant curl of blue-black hair, checked that her skirt was straight, and went through the antechamber with its long, carved wooden seat and the table on which the mail was laid ready for Mother Dorothy's inspection, and tapped on the inner door.

'Come in.' Mother Dorothy's voice didn't sound any sharper than usual, but that was no guarantee.

The parlour beyond had once been a large drawing-room, and the silk embroidered panels, faded but still exquisite, remained on the panelled walls. At the two long windows the original pale curtains hung, their velvet slightly scuffed by the passage of time. A firescreen blocked the hearth above which a plain wooden crucifix hung and the spindly-legged sofas and occasional tables which must once have graced the room had been replaced by a row of filing cabinets, a semi-circle of stools and a flat-topped desk behind which the Prioress sat.

'*Dominus vobiscum.*' She gave the customary greeting.

'*Et cum spirutu tuo.*' Sister Joan knelt briefly as her superior indicated one of the stools.

'You bought the material?' As usual Mother Dorothy dealt first with the practicalities.

'Yes, Mother. I called at the presbytery too. Father Malone has made arrangements for the bishop's coming. He sent his blessing. Sister Jerome gave me a cup of coffee.'

'And which set of photographs did you look at this morning?' Mother Dorothy asked. Evidently she wasn't in trouble then or Mother Dorothy wouldn't have hovered so near a joke.

'Assisi, Mother.' Sister Joan folded her hands and risked a smile.

'That dear man will never recover from the thrill of his pilgrimage,' Mother Dorothy said, also smiling. 'Well we have some news. You know how earnestly we have been praying for new vocations. Well, two young women have applied to stay here for a couple of weeks with a view to entering the order. If both are suitable that means that when Sister Marie and Sister Elizabeth enter the novitiate Sister

Hilaria will have two new postulants to train. It is extremely good news.'

'Yes, indeed.' Sister Joan sat up eagerly, her face bright.

'One of them, Bernadette Fawkes, writes to us from Yorkshire. She encloses a letter of recommendation from her parish priest, which, of course, is not strictly necessary yet, but it shows she is serious in her intention. The other is a Magdalen Cole, who writes from London.'

'Two separate applications.'

'Which I prefer. When two friends turn up, declaring they have a vocation, I am always a trifle wary. So often the stronger personality influences the weaker. Now for the bad news.'

'Bad news?'

'Bad is not accurate – slightly inconvenient would fit better. Miss Cole says in her letter she will be arriving today on the late afternoon train. Miss Fawkes says she will be arriving as soon as I approve her application. She doesn't take her welcome for granted.'

It was clear from her tone that she preferred a touch of diffidence.

'You will approve her application?' Sister Joan queried.

'Yes, of course. I immediately telephoned Miss Fawkes's parish priest and as luck would have it she was there discussing the matter with him. I suggested she might like to come down immediately so that she could arrive at the same time as Miss Cole, and she said that she'd go at once to the station. Apparently she had her case packed in readiness. Her priest rang me back a few minutes ago to inform me she had caught the London train by the skin of her teeth, so she will be here on the same train as Miss Cole though they obviously won't be travelling together. It means that we shall have to prepare the two vacant cells upstairs rather quickly and you will have to take the car into town to meet them both.'

'How will I recognize them?'

'If I were you I'd station myself at the station exit and wait for them to recognize you,' Mother Dorothy said. 'Bernadette

Fawkes is twenty-two. Magdalen Cole doesn't give her age.'

'I'll see they get a good welcome,' Sister Joan said. 'Will they join in with the life of the community?'

'As far as their lay status permits. They will be paying a modest fee for bed and board but they will of course, be guests while they're with us. It will give them the chance to observe the routine of the convent at first hand and help them to decide whether or not the religious life might be for them. As much as we wish for new vocations that is no reason for lowering our standards. I think it might be a nice gesture if we were to put flowers in the two cells and see if Sister Perpetua can provide a couple of hot-water bottles. They may find it cold here at night with no heating.'

They're not the only ones, Sister Joan thought irreverently, as she rose and knelt, saying aloud, 'I'll see about it, Mother. May I be excused now to get on with lunch?'

'Yes, of course. I'll announce the imminent arrival of our two guests at the meal. Thank you, Sister.'

Two intending postulants marked the day as a red letter one. In the hall Sister Joan paused to smile at the prospect. The front door was still open but the sunlight had fled from the lawn beyond. The breeze must have sharpened since there was no other reason for the long shiver that suddenly racked her from head to foot.

Two

Sister Perpetua had started off the soup and cut bread for the cheese sandwiches that accompanied it. Lunch, even on non-fast days, was a modest affair. It matched her own culinary skills, she thought wryly, wondering if her own artistic talents would ever be fully utilized. An occasional painting, a piece of embroidery, were all she had been permitted to do since her entry into the religious life. She knew the reason for it which didn't make it any easier to bear. She took a personal pride in her talents unlike Sister Katharine who produced exquisite lace without thinking for one moment that she achieved anything out of the common run. Personal pride in one's accomplishments wasn't to be encouraged lest it lead to singularity. But oh for the swishing motion of a brush loaded with paint in her fingers!

'Sister, you're spilling the soup!'

Sister Gabrielle, eighty-six years old and proud of every moment of her years, had come from the infirmary where she and Sister Mary Concepta slept and stood, looking triumphant, in the kitchen doorway.

'I'm very sorry, Sister Gabrielle. I was dreaming.'

'You generally are,' Sister Gabrielle remarked. 'I hear we're to have guests.'

'How on earth did you hear that?'

'Mother Dorothy came to tell Sister Mary Concepta and me. She knows we like to be kept informed of events. It will be agreeable to see a couple of new faces here for a while. If they're suitable that could mean a couple of new postulants for Sister Hilaria to train. Sister Marie and Sister Elizabeth ought to have been admitted into the novitiate months ago.'

'Yes. One doesn't like to ask but—'

'Oh, they both said they felt they needed more time in the postulancy,' Sister Gabrielle said. 'As novices they'd come more directly under Mother Dorothy's rules and Sister Hilaria would be quite lost without a couple of postulants to trail after her. Sister Marie and Sister Elizabeth are two very kind-hearted girls.'

'Yes.' Sister Joan wondered if she could have endured to spend longer as lowly postulant out of the kindness of her heart and was glad that she had never had to make the decision.

'That soup,' said Sister Gabrielle, 'will be stone cold.'

'It's gazpacho, Sister.'

'In my experience,' said Sister Gabrielle, stumping back towards the infirmary, 'cold tomato soup is cold tomato soup in any language.'

Sister Joan chuckled as she carried the heavy tureen down the narrow passage and up the stairs. At the head of the staircase the two backsweeping wings of the building were at left and right, with double doors at the head of the stairs leading into the former ballroom which was built out over the back courtyard.

Ballroom was probably an exaggeration in terms since it could never have held more than six couples comfortably, but the two rooms that now occupied the space and were used as dining-room and recreation-room were handsome enough, divided by a further wall with double doors. Setting her tray down on the serving table Sister Joan wished, not for the first time, that the original owners had seen fit to install a dumbwaiter for the convenience of the servants. There was a back staircase but carrying the food up there would still entail a longish trip down the passage that led between the sleeping quarters in the left-hand wing.

The sisters were filing in. Sister Joan hoped that Sister Hilaria, whose absent-mindedness was only matched by her greatness of spirit, had remembered to feed Sister Teresa who had moved back into the postulancy for her year of isolation before her final profession. The novice mistress was entering now, tall and broad shouldered with the prominent eyes of the natural mystic, her two pink-smocked postulants before her, their heads bent within their white poke bonnets.

The announcement that two guests would be arriving later and were to be duly made welcome was made and greeted with small exclamations of pleasure. The prospect of two new postulants was exciting.

'They hope to stay with us for a couple of weeks,' Mother Dorothy was saying, 'so they will have plenty of time to see how we live here. We must make them feel at home without disguising from them that the religious life is not a life of luxury or selfish pleasure. They will sleep in Sister Joan's and Sister Teresa's old cells and join us for meals and recreation and whichever services and spiritual studies they choose. That will be all. Let us give thanks for our food now.'

'Gazpacho,' said Sister Gabriella audibly and looked primly at her plate.

Washing up afterwards, giving Alice a biscuit to make up for having deserted her in the forenoon, Sister Joan found herself trying to imagine what the visitors would look like. The fact that Mother Dorothy had requested that she meet them indicated that she would also be expected to act as guide. Sister Joan, who couldn't have existed for five minutes in a silent order, smiled in anticipation.

At four o'clock she finished washing the windows and went out to polish the car. Polishing the old convent car was like putting a thick coat of make-up on an ageing face. Another six months and they'd have to trade the old jalopy in for something more likely to stop and start at the proper times and not lose bits of its anatomy when it went over a bump in the road. An estate car would be nice, she thought. A Mercedes and a holiday in the Bahamas would also be nice and equally out of reach.

'Are you ready, Sister?' Mother Dorothy had come out. 'Be

sure to bring them straight back here.'

'Yes, of course, Reverend Mother.'

Did the prioress imagine she was going to take them nightclubbing? Sister Joan suppressed a giggle and got into the driving seat.

She must have been mistaken about there being a change in the weather. The sky was a clear bright blue with curls of fleecy white cloud drifting across it and the breeze was mild. The moor looked beautiful in late spring. She would have liked to stop the car and get out and walk around on the springing grass and pick some of the wild flowers that starred it, but if she stopped there was no absolute guarantee that the car would start again without help, so she drove on sedately.

Reaching the station, she parked neatly, bought herself a platform ticket and stationed herself near the exit. There were a few people waiting to meet the train. Others carried luggage and were obviously waiting to board it. Sister Joan felt, as she always felt, a sense of anticipation. As a child she had always looked forward eagerly to train journeys and never felt when she had travelled by car that she had fully participated in an adventure.

The train was approaching. She snapped to attention, a smile ready for the guests. A fairly large number of passengers were alighting, mostly families ready for an early holiday. Some of the children carried buckets and spades and shrimping gear, though the beaches were a good hour's drive off and hardly suitable for digging sand castles. They streamed past, chattering and laughing.

A young woman with a round face and a long braid of dark hair over one shoulder had paused at a little distance, setting down a suitcase and eyeing Sister Joan for a moment before she stepped foward, hand outstretched.

'Would you be waiting for me, Sister?' Her voice was warm and friendly with a slight Yorkshire burr.

'Bernadette Fawkes?' Sister Joan shook hands.

'Father Mulhaney saw me off this morning. Gosh, but that was a rush!' She laughed in an unaffected way. 'One minute

I'm in Leeds and the next I'm in Cornwall. One of the reasons I thought of coming to your convent was because I've never been to this part of the country before, so even if I decide not to be a nun at least I'll have had a bit of a holiday. You're awfully young to be a prioress.'

'Good heavens! I'm not the prioress,' Sister Joan said, amused. 'I'm Sister Joan, acting as lay sister at present because we haven't got a regular one. Mother Dorothy asked me to meet you.'

'Do you take turns being lay sister?' Bernadette enquired.

'No, not usually. A sister decides at her profession if she wishes to be a lay sister or a member of the semi-enclosed community. When it's necessary a sister who is semi-enclosed can take on lay duties for a period but not the other way round.'

'Sounds a bit snobbish to me,' Bernadette said frankly. 'Like first class and second class, you know.'

'Then I explained it badly. Lay sisters do the more practical work that brings them into more contact with the outside, that's all. They're fully professed in every way but their job's different. That's all. Excuse me, but I think I see our other visitor.'

She broke off as a girl, a scarf over her head, a dark coat covering her slim frame, came towards them, suitcase in hand. Under the scarf her features looked blurred, unformed like the features of a young child. Then she raised her head and fixed huge, doe-shaped eyes of a clear and brilliant grey on Sister Joan's face.

'Are you—?' Her voice was soft and clear.

'Sister Joan from the convent, yes. I've been deputed as the welcoming committee. You're Magdalen Cole?'

'Magdalen Cole, yes.' Sister Joan's hand was taken and briefly held.

Pure grey eyes, Sister Joan thought, which was, she had read somewehere, the purest and rarest of eye colours. The long lashes shielding them were dark in contrast to a lock of pale coppery hair as it strayed from the concealing scarf.

'Give me your suitcases,' Sister Joan said briskly. 'Oh, sorry! Magdalen Cole, meet Bernadette Fawkes. She's your fellow guest.'

'I didn't know there were to be two of us,' Magdalen Cole said.

'Neither did I. We could've had a bit of a chat on the way down,' Bernadette Fawkes said. 'You just lead the way, Sister. We can carry our own cases.'

'This way then.' Sister Joan led them through the low tunnel into the car-park. 'I'm afraid the car's on its last legs, poor thing. However it does go! Put your cases in the boot and climb in, won't you?'

Both had climbed into the back seat leaving her in solitary splendour behind the wheel.

'You'll be in time for a cup of tea before we go into chapel,' she said over her shoulder as she started the engine. 'The convent's up on the moor. We turn off onto the track in a moment. Have you been to Cornwall, Miss Cole?'

The girl shook her head mutely.

'That makes two of us,' Bernadette Fawkes said cheerfully.

'Don't worry about the old boneshaker.' Sister Joan had caught a glimpse of Magdalen's strained expression in the driving mirror. 'I'm a good driver. These days I usually ride the convent pony into town if I haven't got a load of stuff to carry back. Her name is Lilith after Adam's first wife but we can't be blamed for that – we inherited the name along with the pony.'

'Do the sisters go often into town?' Magdalen Cole asked.

'Once a month the lay sister – that's me at the moment – goes in to get supplies of rice, pasta, tea, sugar, coffee. We grow our own fruit and vegetables. That's Sister Martha's job and Sister Perpetua, our infirmarian, sells the surplus at market for us. We collect dairy foods from a local farm and the Romanies bring us gifts of fish from time to time.'

She carefully didn't add that it was highly likely some of the fish had been poached.

'You don't eat meat?' Bernadette Fawkes asked.

'Not at all. Will that be a problem for you? If one's health demands it then we do make exceptions for medical reasons.'

'I can live without chops,' Bernadette Fawkes said, laughter in her voice.

'I'm a vegetarian,' the other said primly. 'What's that?' There was a sudden note of alarm in her voice.

'The old school building. It used to be part of the original Tarquin estate so it now belongs to the convent. The local authorities laid on a bus for the kids from outlying districts so the place isn't used now.'

'Then there aren't any neighbours?'

'None within a mile or so.' Sister Joan wondered at the anxiety in Magdalen Cole's soft voice. 'There's a housing estate a couple of miles past the convent, and the permanent Romany settlement over the hill but that's about all. Here we are!'

They drove slowly through the gates, Alice's excited yelping reaching them as they turned into the cobbled yard.

'That's Alice. She's an Alsatian but very friendly.' Sister Joan unclipped her seat belt. 'Leave your luggage in the car for now. Someone will take it up for you. Alice, down! You're supposed to be a guard dog. We'll go round to the front door and introduce you to Mother Dorothy.'

'It's very posh,' Bernadette Fawkes said as they rounded the corner again.

'The Tarquins were posh and built accordingly,' Sister Joan said. 'This is the main hall with the prioress's parlour there on the left and the door on the right leading to the chapel wing. The door at the foot of the stairs leads to the infirmary and the kitchen. The lay cells are off the kitchen and the other cells directly above. You'll soon find your way around.'

'Who were the Tarquins?' Bernadette Fawkes enquired.

'The local squires. They sold off their property to our order and the family died out. Come and meet Mother Dorothy. We elect a new prioress every five years so Mother Dorothy still has nearly three years of her term of office to go.'

She went through the antechamber, tapped on the door, opened it in response to Mother Dorothy's invitation, ushered the visitors within and, at a glance from her superior, went out again. The prioress would wish to make her own instinctive evaluation without anyone else being present.

It was ten minutes before the parlour door opened again and Mother Dorothy emerged, a short, spare, middle-aged figure beside the willowy slenderness of the younger girls.

'Take Bernadette and Magdalen to the kitchen for a cup of tea and then show them over the main house before chapel,' she instructed. 'They both agree that Christian names will be more informal. Sister Joan will explain our routine to you but you're not bound to join in anything. And you mustn't feel you have to confine yourself to the encosure while you're here. There are some very pleasant moorland walks.'

'Thank you, Reverend Mother Prioress.' Magdalen had bowed her head submissively.

'Mother Dorothy will do. Thank you, Sister.' The prioress re-entered her parlour and closed the door firmly.

'She's a bit of a Tartar that one,' Bernadette said in an undertone as Sister Joan went ahead into the kitchen passage.

'Sometimes,' said Sister Joan, flashing a grin over her shoulder, 'she needs to be!'

'There you are!' Sister Perpetua greeted them with her usual impatience as they went into the big, stone-flagged kitchen. 'I've boiled the kettle twice. Now which of you is which?'

Sister Joan made the necessary introductions.

'Bernadette and Magdalen.' Sister Perpetua handed round mugs. 'Two decent Catholic names for a change. Take off your coats and make yourself comfortable. Sister Martha took up the cases.'

Bernadette pulled off her windcheater to reveal a dark green sweater which picked up the fleck in her tweed skirt. Magdalen was also wearing green, a shapeless dress of a muddy olive colour, both execrable. Her headscarf was untied with what Sister Joan interpreted as marked reluctance to reveal shining coils of coppery hair with strands escaping from their pins to feather her face. The piled hair looked too heavy for the frail neck.

'Well, I've red hair myself,' Sister Perpetua remarked, pulling at a greying strand. 'It was never that pretty though.'

'It's just hair,' Magdalen said. She sounded as if she resented the compliment.

The tea was drunk, Sister Perpetua thanked, and Sister Joan stood up, sounding in her own ears slightly over-hearty as she said, 'It'll be a quick tour. We have chapel in fifteen minutes. Let's go upstairs and I'll show you where you'll be sleeping. This way.'

She led the way into the main hall again and up the staircase, pointing out the exquisite carving on the balustrade and feeling rather like a tour guide at a stately home. Bernadette was looking about her with unabashed awe. Magdalen made little noises of approbation but her face never woke into animation, her voice remained blurred and soft. Either she had no personality at all or she was concealing it behind a bland mask.

'We have seven cells over the Prioress's parlour and the kitchen wing,' Sister Joan said, reminding herself that first impressions didn't always count. 'Sisters Martha, David, Perpetua and Katharine along this side and this is where you'll be sleeping, next to Mother Dorothy's cell. This is Sister Teresa's cell but she's in seclusion over at the postulancy until her final profession and this one used to be mine, but since I became acting lay sister I sleep in one of the two cells leading off the kitchen.'

'It's very nice,' Magdalen said, obediently entering Sister Teresa's cell. 'Nice' seemed an odd word to use about the rectangle of whitewashed walls, the small white-curtained window, the single bed with its dark blanket, the shelf on which books could be ranged but which now held a glass vase with flowers in it, the hooks at the back of the door where garments could be hung, the two-drawer locker for more intimate garments, the basin and wash jug on the bare wooden floor.

'If you'd like to unpack,' she said aloud, 'and then come down to chapel? I'll wait for you in the main hall.'

Leaving them to it she went downstairs again as Sister Perpetua approached.

'They seem like pleasant girls.' The infirmarian paused to exchange a few words.

'Yes. Yes, they do.'

'Mind you, they'll both be on their best behaviour,' Sister Perpetua was continuing. 'The red-haired one, Magdalen, seems very shy.'

Shy. Sister Joan considered the word. Shy sounded wrong. Reserved. Inhibited. Those were the words she would have chosen herself.

'I'd better go and give Mother Dorothy a hand. She's been telephoning most of the afternoon,' Sister Perpetua said. 'Trying to find a few legal ways of making some money. It seems a pity that we have to pay bills, doesn't it?'

'Especially when they get bigger all the time,' Sister Joan agreed.

Shortage of funds was a perennial problem. The rule allowed nuns to work outside the enclosure if it was necessary but it was difficult even for lay people to find work these days. Produce from the gardens was sold cheaply in the market place and Sister Katharine did well with her lace and needlework. Sister David worked on translations and was compiling a series of short books for children on the saints, dealing with them in alphabetical order, but no publisher had yet been found.

Mother Dorothy came out of the parlour.

'Nothing to do, Sister Joan?' Her eyebrows had risen slightly.

'The guests are getting ready for chapel, Reverend Mother.' Sister Joan automatically straightened up, reflecting not for the first time that Mother Dorothy had that effect on most people.

'I'm sure I can count on you to show them round and make

them welcome.' Mother Dorothy's tone had mellowed slightly. 'It is never easy for lay people when they come into such a different environment.'

'No, it isn't.' Sister Joan's mind flew back to the first time she had entered the mother house in London and breathed in for the first time the scent of beeswax, incense and soap that had been the prevailing perfume in every convent she had entered since.

'Yes, very pleasant girls,' Mother Dorothy repeated. She seemed to be following her own private train of thought since she added a moment later in a voice that didn't seem to be directed at anyone in particular, 'Something doesn't fit.'

'Mother?' Sister Joan looked at her.

'Nothing, Sister. You had better go and hurry them up.'

Mother Dorothy went back into the parlour and closed the door.

It wasn't like the prioress to be obtuse. Sister Joan frowned after her for a moment, then turned as the two visitors came down the stairs. Magdalen had resumed her dark headscarf. Bernadette had made a token effort by tying a handkerchief over her head, beneath which her long braid of dark hair swung like a rope.

'You said we had no neighbours,' Magdalen said.

'We haven't – not near ones anyway.'

'Through the small window in the bathroom. I caught sight of another house.'

'Another—? oh, that's the postulancy,' Sister Joan said, trying not to notice that the girl's hands were clenched into fists. 'It used to be the old dower house so it serves very well for the postulants. Sister Hilaria is novice mistress and we have two postulants – Sister Marie and Sister Elizabeth who are ready now to join the novitiate. They have lunch and supper over here and come to chapel and spiritual instruction but they sleep over in the postulancy and have their own studies and recreation there. We had better go into chapel if you're ready. There's cheese salad tonight and I believe Sister Perpetua has made one of her steamed jam puddings.'

In the chapel she ushered them to a couple of spare seats and went to her own place. It was not a benediction proper but a simple service of prayer and song conducted by the prioress. Wednesdays and Saturdays were the days on which either Father Malone or Father Stephens came up to conduct the full service. She wondered what they would make of the two visitors. Would they too feel that something didn't fit?

Chapel was followed by supper, the most eagerly awaited meal of the day since it was the most substantial. The community filed out, Sister Joan lingering to wait for the guests.

'We have supper now and then recreation,' she said. 'We chat and play draughts and Scrabble and knit or sew. It's a lively period.'

'Do we have to go to it?' Magdalen asked.

'No, of course not. You can go up to the library over the chapel and borrow a book if you like. Sister David is our librarian and she likes us to sign the book there when we take anything out – there's quite a wide selection. Or you can help me with the dishes if you're feeling self-sacrificing.'

'I'll help with the dishes,' Magdalen said.

'Bernadette?' Sister Joan looked at her.

'I'll be self-sacrificing tomorrow,' Bernadette said brightly. 'I'd like to go to recreation, Sister.'

'Fine. Let's go up to supper then.'

Shepherding them up the stairs she wished that she could look forward to Magdalen's prospective company a little more. The girl was unsure of herself, wanting to create a good impression, that was all.

'Sister, can you take up the bread? I've done everything else but I have to help Sister Mary Concepta upstairs,' Sister Martha asked as she approached.

'Sister, I'm sorry! That was my responsibility.' Sister Joan dived back through to the kitchen, thinking ruefully that she must be getting old if she couldn't keep more than one thing in her head at a time, and picked up the bread basket and the jug of dressing.

Alice growled suddenly, deep in her throat, raising her head from the basket where she was curled.

'What is it, girl?' Sister Joan put down the dishes and went to the kichen window. In the courtyard a soft twilight was stealing in and the shadows were growing longer. Nothing moved but a restless whinny came from the stable.

Standing at the window wasn't going to achieve much. Sister Joan opened the door and said loudly, 'Hello! is anybody there?'

There was only the echo of her own voice. The breeze had freshened, blustering round the corner in a flurry of dust motes.

'Is there someone there?' She took another couple of steps forward, the breeze lifting the edge of her veil.

Alice had put her head down again for a nap. Probably she had been chasing a stray rabbit in her sleep. Sister Joan retreated, closing the door with a little bang, and sliding the bolt.

'Good dog, Alice.' She patted the dog and took bread and dressing up the stairs.

The community was in place at the long table, Sister Hilaria with her charges, the prioress at the head of the table.

The latter raised an eyebrow as Sister Joan panted in but refrained from reciting the grace until she was in her place. At the other side of the table the two visitors sat together, Magdalen still wearing her headscarf.

'We are fortunate to have the opportunity of welcoming two visitors,' Mother Dorothy said when Grace was done. 'Bernadette and Magdalen have asked that we call them by their Christian names while they are here. Of course there is a possibility that one or both of them may join us later as fellow religious, but whether they do or not I know we'll all do everything possible to make them feel at home. Sister Joan, though we have guests we must keep to the routine.'

'Yes, Mother Dorothy,' Sister Joan said.

Nobody would be more pleased than herself when a full-time lay sister could be found. She did her best but it was a difficult position to hold between the demands of the spiritual and the duties of what amounted to a full-time housekeeper. There would never again be a lay sister like Sister Margaret, poised so delicately between heaven and earth.*

At supper one of the sisters read aloud from a book dealing with the spiritual. Sister Katharine was at the lectern this evening, her gentle face animated as she read the story of St Mary Magdalen – a compliment to her namesake who sat, steadily eating, her head bent, her slim shoulders hunched as if she awaited a blow.

The reading drew to a close. Sister Katharine took her place at the end of the table. The rest of the community filed into the recreation-room, apart from Sister Hilaria and the two postulants, who returned to the postulancy for their own period of relaxation before the final blessing of the day.

'Here's your salad, Sister Katharine.' Sister Joan set it down and motioned towards the side table. 'The pudding's still nice and hot. I'll clear away later. I enjoyed the reading tonight.'

Sister Katharine's delicately pretty face flushed becomingly.

'It was Mother Dorothy's idea,' she said. 'Tomorrow I'm to read something about St Bernadette of Lourdes.'

'And steal Father Malone's thunder? Shame on you!' Sister Joan picked up the heavy tray and looked round. 'Oh, where did Magdalen go?'

'To recreation perhaps?' Sister Katharine suggested.

'She said she preferred to help me in the kitchen – oh well she's entitled to change her mind.'

Glancing towards the adjoining door, she decided not to interrupt. She would probably get on faster alone.

Going down into the kitchen she unbolted the door and let Alice out for a run. Mother Dorothy had been adamant that pets had no place in a convent and had only allowed Alice to remain on condition that she was trained as a reliable guard

* See *Vow of Chastity*

dog. So far her training had been somewhat desultory and far from showing suspicion of any stranger she welcomed every comer as a long lost member of her pack.

The evening had chilled. Sister Joan shivered slightly as she rolled up her sleeves and tackled the dishes, grateful for the hot water and the warmth still emitted from the cooker and the banked up fire that fed the boiler. For her one of the great deprivations of the religious life had been the complete absence of heating save in kitchen and infirmary. There were times even now when she thought wistfully of a sofa drawn up to a blazing log fire and a good novel and a box of chocolates to while away the time.

Outside Alice began barking to be let in.

'Alice! Here, girl!' Sister Joan opened the back door and whistled.

The dog came in like an arrow shot by a very competent archer and bounded round as if she had been exiled for days.

'Silly girl! When you're trained you'll have to patrol the grounds at night.' Sister Joan set down the dinner of biscuits and gravy to which Alice immediately applied herself as if she hadn't been charming titbits out of Sister Perpetua all day.

The dishes dried and the cloths scalded, she slipped across the yard to check on Lilith who greeted her with a nuzzling nose.

'Here's your supper.' Sister Joan offered the nightly treat, checked on feed and water, and resolved that with the improvement in the weather she'd make time to exercise the pony more often.

Lilith was no youngster but she still relished a good gallop from time to time.

'And so do I?' Sister Joan questioned aloud and laughed as she bolted the stable door, patted the old jalopy in the yard, and went back inside.

There were still ten minutes of recreation left. It was Sister David's task as sacristan to check on the chapel but, since she also combined the duties of secretary with her work as translator, recently she had allowed a few practical matters to slip her mind and Sister Joan had fallen into the habit of checking up without advertising the fact. The last thing that Mother Dorothy would welcome was the emergence of another sister as dreamy as Sister Hilaria.

'She is a great soul and may be permitted a little wool gathering,' she had once informed Sister Joan, 'but we are not blessed with her particular gifts, Sister, so it behoves us to keep our feet on the ground.'

She had not, of course, been talking about Sister David but scolding Sister Joan for absentmindedly putting bicarbonate of soda instead of cornflour in the sponge cake. The memory of that made her grin ruefully again as she bolted the back door and went across the main hall to the chapel wing.

In the chapel the sanctuary light burned as it always burned with a steady, deep crimson flame that cast a rosy glow over the main altar above which the carved figure of Christ brooded, haloed by the first starlight piercing the circular window behind. A slender shape stood just beyond the Lady Altar, looking up the narrow stairs as if deciding whether or not to mount. Magdalen had obviously gone exploring by herself, but there was something about her strained, listening attitude that seemed to beg for company.

'Is there anything I can—?' Sister Joan gulped as Magdalen swung round, her face alight with panic.

That was ironic, Sister Joan thought. Why did Magdalen look so terrified when she was the one holding the open flick knife?

Three

'I'm sorry, Sister.' The knife was withdrawn as swiftly as it had appeared. 'You startled me.'

'Evidently.' Sister Joan took a grip on herself. 'Isn't it illegal to carry a flick knife these days?'

'Sometimes one is followed,' Magdalen said.

'Even so.' Sister Joan hesitated, wondering what on earth to do. There was nothing in the rule about carrying weapons. 'In the city I imagine it can be quite dangerous for a lone woman but here there's really nothing to worry about. The only person who's liable to trail after you is Luther from the Romany camp. He's a bit simple in the head but completely harmless. Perhaps you'd better let me take care of it?'

'I feel safer with some protection,' Magdalen said.

'Look, we can go into town tomorrow and buy a personal alarm if you like,' Sister Joan suggested. 'One of those that screams if you press it. Believe me, but we'd all come running.'

'I won't come into town,' Magdalen said, 'but I'd be grateful for the alarm. I can give you the money for it now.'

She dug in the pocket of her dress and thrust a number of notes into Sister Joan's hand.

'I'll see you get a receipt,' Sister Joan said, wondering what on earth she was letting herself in for. 'Honestly you've no need to worry.'

'Is the library up there?' Magdalen indicated the stairs.

'The library and the storerooms, yes. Did you want to borrow a book? We have lights out at nine-thirty but, of course, you may keep yours on to read if you wish.'

'I'll do as the community does. Are the windows up there locked?'

'No, they don't have locks,' Sister Joan said. 'Look, if you're worried about any burglars there's no need to be! We leave the outside door to the chapel open all the time because we like to feel that anyone in need of spiritual comfort can come in to pray at any hour of the day or night, but we lock the inner door that divides this wing from the hall last thing at night, and though anyone coming into the chapel could go up to the library the upper wing is blocked off from the main wing. They'd have to break down a brick wall in order to get through to the rest of us. Shall we go and start clearing up in the kitchen or would you like to join the others at recreation?'

'I'll help you, Sister.'

The panic, the hint of violence were gone. Magdalen genuflected to the altar and went meekly out, pausing only to bless herself from the holy-water stoup.

Something had frightened the girl, frightened her so badly that she carried a knife with which to defend herself. Her drab appearance, so much at variance with her delicate patrician colouring, her beautifully manicured nails, her refusal to contemplate a trip into town, her checking out of neighbouring buildings and of locks all pointed one way. Magdalen Cole was hiding. From an enemy or from the law? Sister Joan, wiping up dishes as the other washed them, was visited by doubt.

Ought she to tell Mother Dorothy immediately about what had transpired or should she keep her own counsel for the moment, watch and wait? Magdalen might be having delusions or choosing a rather odd way in which to make herself seem interesting to the community. For the time being she would wait. She would also, she decided firmly, get hold of that flick knife as quickly as possible.

The chapel bell rang the signal for the last prayers of the day. Magdalen wiped her hands on the kitchen towel and fell in behind Sister Joan as they returned to the chapel for the night office and the blessing that marked the start of the grand silence which lasted until Sister Joan, in her capacity as lay sister, heaved herself out of bed at 5 a.m. the next morning to wake the community with the cry of 'Christ is risen', repeated at the door of every cell. For the next few hours she could put the problem of the visitor at the back of her mind and sleep.

Or not sleep! Two hours later she sat up in bed, thumped her pillow and decided that she must have been infected by Magdalen's apprehension, since she needed to check that the locks were all secure. Pulling on her dressing-gown and slippers she padded into the kitchen, where Alice, asleep in her basket, opened one eye and promptly fell asleep again.

The back door and window were firmly bolted as was the window of the empty cell adjoining her own. She went down the passage, hearing a rhythmic snoring from the infirmary where the two old sisters slept, past the dispensary with its bottles of coltsfoot cough mixture and jars of herbs, into the wide entrance hall.

A low wattage bulb burned in the standard lamp in the corner. The door leading into the chapel wing was bolted as it customarily was. She stepped across and drew the bolt back softly. When one couldn't sleep, something that happened only rarely to herself, a few minutes in church calmed one's spirit. She opened the door, closed it and went along the unlit corridor towards the chapel door where the perpetual lamp threw a beam of comfort.

Lowering herself into her usual seat she closed her eyes, letting the peace lap round her. Perhaps the wisest course of action at this stage was to keep silent, to persuade Magdalen to give up the knife, and trust that the conventual routine, the friendliness of the community, and the Presence in the chapel itself would remove the fear that clearly affected the young woman.

Someone was walking about overhead. The soft tread tread of feet over bare boards beat a regular rhythm over her head. Sister Joan's eyes flew open and she sat upright, the last faint desire for sleep disappearing. One of the other sisters? Surely not. When anyone found sleep impossible the chapel was the first recourse, not the darkened library and storerooms above.

There was nothing worth stealing in the upstairs storey. The only items of value were here in the chapel. An ordinary thief could come in, load his bag with silver candlesticks and chalice, use the small key to unlock the monstrance with its star panels of silver and pearl hidden behind the curtain of the sanctuary. Not an ordinary thief, she corrected herself mentally. Only a man without sensitivity would rob a chapel. And this chapel hadn't been robbed. Everything was in place, dim and shadowed by the night.

Rising, her slippers making no noise on the carpet, she moved to the Lady-altar where the narrow staircase spiralled upwards into blackness. Had there been a door at the top she might have crept up and bolted it but the stairs came out on to a square landing with library and storerooms opening off it.

If she went and woke up the rest of the community there would be general panic and if she tried to rouse Sister Perpetua who was the tallest and most vigorous of the sisters the infirmarian would make so much noise getting into the chapel that any intruder would be alerted.

Sister Joan picked up an empty candlestick from the altar, breathed a silent prayer to Our Lady of Compassion whose plaster statue held a smiling Baby Jesus, and went up the spiral stairs, wishing she had confiscated the flick knife.

A thin pencil of light moved across the landing past the open doors of the storerooms. Sister Joan hesitated, then stepped within the library and stood, close pressed against the half-open door, listening. The tread tread of the pacing feet was clear up here. She listened for some sound of breathing but there was none, though that was probably because her own heart was beating like a drum in her ears.

Someone was coming closer. She heard the footsteps stop,

held her breath as the pencil of light steadied, then moved slowly across the landing. A shadow, grotesque and batlike, filled the wall, swelled and diminished. Someone – something? went past down the stairs in a swirl of blackness, and the light was gone before she could cry out.

She took a couple of deep breaths and eased herself away from the door frame, the candlestick jerking nervously in her hand. Below a door closed softly, galvanizing her into action. Which way had the intruder gone? Through the door that led into the main hall and thence to the rest of the convent? Please God, no!

In the chapel she stood for a fraction of a second, not sure which way to turn. Then she was opening the inner door just as the long pencil of light shone outside one of the windows, making the diamond panes glitter. Whoever had paced the storerooms had gone through the outer door. Sister Joan turned and ran down the narrow passage, her hand shooting home the bolt on the outer door. Should any poor soul need prayer or spiritual comfort this night they would have to sit on the doorstep until she came at dawn to unlock the entrance door.

The candlestick was still in her hand. She looked at it stupidly before moving back into the chapel and replacing it on the Lady-altar. Her legs were shaking as if she had been running for miles. Lowering herself gingerly to the floor she rested her head against the wooden base of the altar and tried to collect her thoughts. Someone had been hanging round the convent earlier. She remembered Alice's warning growl, the high snickering whinny of the pony. Whoever had been there had waited until all was quiet and then entered the chapel by way of the outside door and gone upstairs. Clearly they had found the inner door locked and sought another way into the convent. For the first time Sister Joan blessed the snobbishness of the Tarquin family who had blocked off the access between family rooms and staff quarters.

She rose at last, fright giving way to weariness and made her way through the inner door, bolting it carefully, before padding across the hall into the antechamber beyond which was the prioress's parlour. The bay windows here were always locked at night but it would do no harm to check them. She did so, her eyes straying to the dark lawn outside, but no pencil of light pierced the gloom. The intruder had gone, swirled away into blackness as if they had been no more than the figment of a nightmare.

By the time she had reached her cell again she was aching with weariness. If the intruder returned then at least every door would be bolted now. She pulled off her dressing-gown, stepped out of her slippers, and was asleep as her head hit the pillow.

Habit woke her only a few minutes after time. She dressed hastily, splashed her face with cold water, tugged a comb through her short mop of black curls, pinned her short veil and went to open the inner and outer doors of the chapel. The early morning air had a soft grey quality like the inside of an oyster. Dew sparkled on the turf beyond the door and the trees that bordered the path rustled in a rising breeze. On the step lay a red rose, its petals still tightly curled, its stem stripped of thorns, only the little cluster of leaves holding a faint prickliness.

A rose before summer had unfolded all its blossoms? Stooping to pick it up she held it for a moment, its heady perfume reaching her through the cool damp of dawn.

It certainly hadn't come from the convent garden. Sister Martha had mentioned only the other day that she guessed her roses would be slow this year. Sister Teresa's white rosebuds would have to come from a local florist. This was a hothouse flower, one most carefully chosen to bloom a day or two after it had been received.

She took it back into the chapel and put it into the vase on the Lady-altar with the soft mass of grey-green catkins already there. At least the rose had solved one problem for her. Burglars didn't arrive bearing the gift of a flower. There was no need as yet to alarm the community with her story. She would make sure the outer door of the chapel was locked and double check the window fastenings every night from now on. It would be easy enough to unbolt the door first thing in the mornings without any of the community being the wiser. And she would do her utmost to gain Magdalen's confidence and find out what that enigmatic young woman could tell her about any of this.

Moving briskly and feeling more herself again now that she had some plan of action she picked up the bell and went up the main staircase, ringing the clapper, and raising her voice in the morning greeting,

'Christ is risen!'

'Thanks be to God!'

One by one came the answering voices. The normal routine of the day had begun. Now there was the morning meditation from which she was excused early in order to get the bread cut and the coffee ready for the simple breakfast that came after mass. It was Father Malone who would offer mass this morning. No doubt he'd bring another batch of photographs with him. Her lips curved as she hurried downstairs to let Alice out.

'And some guard dog you are!' she scolded affectionately. 'Not a peep out of you all night long!'

Alice wriggled joyously, wagging her tail with delight, as she was patted, then bounding out with a series of barks designed to convey her opinion of the morning. She really ought to start her training soon, Sister Joan thought. Nobody in the convent had sufficient experience or time to see about it. She would ask Detective Sergeant Mill how to go about it the next time she saw him. And that, she decided, would be as soon as possible.

Magdalen, wearing a neat grey dress, a white scarf hiding her hair, came into chapel as if she belonged there. Her clothes were almost indistinguishable from the grey habits and white veils all around her. From the back she looked exactly like a member of the community. Sister Joan preferred Bernadette's bright red sweater and pleated skirt.

There was no time to speculate. Sister Joan, slipping out to complete the preparations for breakfast, wondered wryly how many lay people imagined that nuns did nothing but pray all day. They ought to see Sister Martha lugging a sack of potatoes or Sister Katharine struggling with the laundry.

Breakfast was eaten standing, the last of the stored apples being added to the dry bread and coffee that comprised the meal. Father Malone had joined them as usual, shaking hands cordially with the visitors and clearly anxious to display the sheaf of photographs he just happened to have in his pocket. This morning they were of Knock, a place of pilgrimage dear to his Irish heart.

'Mother Dorothy, may I have leave to go into town again?' she asked. 'There are a few things I forgot to get yesterday.'

'If you wish.' Thankfully the prioress didn't ask what things were needed.

'I'll ride Lilith in,' Sister Joan said.

There were still the dishes to be washed and the passages swept before she was free to leave. Rather to her relief she saw Bernadette and Magdalen going off with Sister Perpetua, very likely to chat with the old ladies.

Lilith, saddled and led out, twisted round her head and gave a look of astonishment as if the prospect of a ride two days in succession was altogether too much for her pony brain to assimilate.

It was a lovely morning, the pearl of dawn warmed into gold by the rising sun. Perhaps it was a trifle too warm for the season. When the temperature rose in late spring it often betokened a wet summer.

'Enjoy what's here,' she admonished herself, mounting up. 'Rain can be very refreshing too.'

Riding down the track with the moor billowing around her she had leisure at last to reflect on the events of the previous night. Someone had been hanging around the convent. Later after the community had retired for the night that same person (for there surely hadn't been two trespassers?) had entered the chapel and, finding the inner door locked, had mounted to the storey above in the hope of finding an entrance there. And when they had left, alerted no doubt by the consciousness that someone else had arrived, they had left behind that exquisite rose. Men who left roses didn't usually require to be fended off with flick knives, she thought frowningly. On the other hand a lover might well feel desperate if his girl announced her intention of going into a convent.

She had neared the schoolhouse and, from force of habit, glanced in that direction. To her surprise the door was open and, alarmed and curious, she dismounted and went over to look inside just as Father Stephens emerged, a pile of blankets over his arm.

'Good morning, Father. What on earth's going on?' she demanded.

'Good morning, Sister Joan. We're getting the schoolhouse ready,' he returned.

'For what?'

'Mother Dorothy has rented it to us – to Father Malone that is,' he explained.

'You're going to open the school again?' Pleasure brightened her voice.

'We are to have a lodger here for a year,' Father Stephens said. 'A hermit.'

'I didn't know there were any these days.'

'Oh, occasionally a particular soul needs solitude and silence,' Father Stephens said with that little smile of conscious learning that was the most irritating thing about him.

'Mother Dorothy never said.'

'It was all arranged rather hastily by telephone,' he said. 'Last evening. When we received word that someone wished for a small place suitable for an anchorage we were quite at a loss until Father Malone remembered the schoolhouse. Mother Dorothy agreed to the rental at a very modest fee and I'm here to fix it up a little.'

Behind the building Sister Joan noticed the presbytery car for the first time.

'Do you need any help?' she enquired.

'Not at the moment, thank you. I have a list of necessities here and if our lodger requires anything else he has only to ask. I daresay that Reverend Mother Prioress will be announcing the arrival some time today, since he will probably be attending mass at the convent chapel. It is rather exciting to have the prospect of a hermit on the doorstep, don't you think?'

Sister Joan could have listed more exciting events but she nodded politely.

'I'd better get on. If you do need anything, Father, you know where to come.'

'Indeed I do. Thank you, Sister.' He went back inside.

So another newcomer was arriving unexpectedly, she mused, as she climbed back on to Lilith's broad back. The district was becoming quite crowded. Father Malone hadn't mentioned the matter at breakfast but then he had been wrapped up in his pictures of Knock.

She rode on, wondering suddenly if the hermit had a fancy for red roses. One thing was certain. She would take a very close look at him at the first opportunity.

When she reached the main street she dismounted, led the pony into the alley and tethered her there. Lilith looked round vainly for a patch of grass on which to graze and, finding only paving stones, sent her a look of hurt reproach.

'I won't be too long, girl.' Sister Joan patted her and turned back into the street, slowing her pace as she walked up it.

Where did one buy personal alarms? It wasn't something she had ever needed to purchase. There was a small electrical shop on one corner but she doubted very much if they stocked what she wanted.

'If we don't stop meeting like this, Sister, people will begin to talk,' Detective Sergeant Mill said at her shoulder.

'Good morning, Detective Sergeant Mill. How nice to see you!'

'Opportune certainly,' he said. 'I was very insensitive in my remarks yesterday, and it's bothered me since. I might not see much point in becoming – what do you call it? – a bride of Christ? but that's no excuse for being sarcastic. I hope you'll accept my apology.'

'Accepted.' She held out her hand with a smile. 'Your own situation had cast a cloud over your thinking, that's all. I hope things improve for you.'

'There's no law against hoping,' he said with a slight shrug. 'What brings you into town again so soon?'

'I want to buy a personal alarm,' she said.

'For your own protection?' His dark eyebrows had risen slightly. 'I never set you down as the nervous type – or is it the prospect of the new-age travellers?'

'It's not for me,' Sister Joan said. 'It's for a – an acquaintance of mine. She would feel much safer if she had one of those alarms. The sort that screams when you press it.'

'They're not very likely to stock them here,' he said. 'We might have a couple down at the station. The manufacturers often send us a model to check that as a deterrant it lies within the law. Come along and we'll see.'

Providence might be fickle but she generally produced Detective Sergeant Mill when he was needed. Sister Joan trotted along at his side, feeling more cheerful than before.

'Come in, Sister.' He ushered her past the desk sergeant into his office. It was an office that gave no clue about the personality of the man who occupied it. There were a few posters on the buff-coloured walls, a nondescript carpet, a flat-topped desk with a swivel chair behind it, papers piled high on the tops of the filing cabinets, a small coffee-maker in one corner, two straight-backed chairs placed at an angle to the desk.

The only personal item in the room was the photograph of two smiling little boys on the desk. Sister Joan glanced at them. His sons must be about twelve and ten by now. The photograph was about five years old. Perhaps he kept it as a memento of the time when he and their mother had still been in love.

'Take a seat, Sister. Coffee?'

'No, thank you.' She seated herself neatly on the chair.

He pressed the bell at the side of the desk and a constable came in.

'Do we have any of those personal rape alarms left?' Detective Sergeant Mill asked.

'Yes, sir. We have one left from the free samples.' The constable had a poker face that betrayed nothing. He merely nodded, said,

'Right, sir,' and went out again without seeming to notice Sister Joan.

'I didn't know that any alarms were outside the law,' she said.

'Canisters of C.S. gas are,' he informed her. 'In France they're legal but not here. Sometimes I think the dice are loaded in the criminal's favour. Ah! thank you, Grant.'

The constable put the small box on the desk, saluted and went out.

'This is quite neat.' Detective Sergeant Mill opened the box. 'It runs on battery, and can be carried easily in the palm of the hand. There's a wrist strap so nobody can knock it away, and when you squeeze on the red spot here – try it.'

Sister Joan did so and hastily removed her finger as an earpiercing scream rent the air.

'It certainly works,' she said, seeing with amusement that a couple of helmeted heads had come into view behind the glazed upper half of the door.

'It's not infallible,' he said. 'The noise stops when you remove the pressure but by the time an attacker has figured out where the din is coming from the neighbours will certainly have been alerted. If you feel safer carrying it then have it by all means.'

'It's not for me,' Sister Joan said, and saw from the slight twitch of his lips that he didn't believe it for a moment. 'And, of course, I'll pay.'

'It was a free sample. Compliments of the Force. Can I get you anything else while you're here? A shot-gun perhaps?'

'This will do very nicely,' she said, suppressing a grin.

'Anyway I doubt if I could shoot straight. Thank you.'

'Are you really worried about these new-age travellers?' he enquired, rising as she rose. 'Most of them are fairly harmless, you know.'

'They just mess up the countryside from what I've heard. No, I'm not scared of them. Thank you again.'

'I'll see you out.' He moved to the door. 'There's nothing wrong up at the convent, I hope?'

'Nothing that can't be handled,' Sister Joan said, hoping that it was true. 'Oh, one thing, if you please! If one wished to buy a red rose here in town where would one go? Our regular florist would have to send away for out of season blooms if we required something that wasn't growing in the enclosure garden.'

Detective Sergeant Mill had stopped to give her a long thoughtful look. After a moment he said, 'So there's nothing you can't handle going on at the convent? Rape alarms and an unseasonable red rose. You're piquing my curiosity, Sister.'

'And it isn't really up to me to satisfy it yet,' she said. 'I will if and when I can, of course.'

'Of course.' His mouth twitched again. 'If you're enquiring after red roses, Sister, there's a specialist rose grower a few miles up the line. They show at Chelsea and other important events. Name of Tregarron.'

'Thank you, Detective Sergeant Mill. You've been very helpful.'

She went off aware that he had paused on the steps of the station to look after her. It would, of course, have been possible to tell him about the flick knife and the intruder, but there was no point in getting Magdalen into trouble if her knife could be coaxed away from her, and if she mentioned an intruder he would insist on sending a couple of policemen up to keep an eye on the place. Sister Joan guessed that the man who had left a red rose might come again and preferred not to have the local constabulary barring the way.

The streets seemed suddenly more crowded. Untying Lilith she heard an impatient voice.

'Move on and stop cluttering up the place! Oh, beg pardon, Sister, I didn't realize it was you!'

Constable Petrie, blinking sun glare out of his eyes, had blushed hotly as she drew nearer.

'I won't be cluttering up the place for long,' she said, mounting up.

'Oh, it's not you, Sister,' he said hastily. 'We've a queue of vans, cars, lorries and the Lord knows what else stretching back for nearly a mile, holding up all the regular traffic.'

'The new-age travellers are here.'

'And I wish they'd move on or go back where they came from,' he said in heartfelt tones. 'Not that I'd wish them on anyone else but they have to go somewhere, I suppose. Before we know where we are they'll be selling crack and holding rave ups outside the Town Hall.'

'I'm sure you'll cope with it all,' she said, raising her hand in salute as she walked Lilith off, holding the reins tightly since the pony showed a tendency to dash off.

There were a couple of extra policemen out, chivvying on the traffic which was threatening to create a bottleneck. Sister Joan weaved a way between them, trying not to look shocked at the condition of some of the vehicles. In comparison the convent car looked in pristine state.

Some of the vans had garish pictures and slogans painted over them. There seemed to be a horde of shaggy-haired children hanging out of the window and the barking of dogs followed her as she gained a clear space and rode Lilith at a faster pace on to the moorland track.

Perhaps she was getting middle-aged and narrow-minded. There was no law that said people had to go on living in the same place for ever, and many of those who roamed in their vans were, she was certain, decent people. Some of them were probably Catholics which meant Father Malone would have his hands full.

'Sister Joan!' A man whose ear-ring and red neckerchief betokened the old-style Romany was hailing her.

'Padraic Lee! How good to see you!' She reined Lilith in

with alacrity. 'Sister Perpetua was saying the other day that she hadn't seen you for weeks.'

'She'll be missing her supplies of fresh fish, I daresay.' He pushed his cap to the back of his head and grinned up at her. 'I've been away for a bit.'

'What was the charge?'

'No charge at all, Sister! You talk as if I was a criminal,' he said in injured innocence. 'No, my good wife went into hospital for a while, and since I wanted to be near her I took myself and the kids up to Birmingham to stay with her brother and his wife for a bit. He's doing a nice line in second-hand cars so I helped him out there while we waited. Got back yesterday.'

'How is your wife?' she enquired.

'A new woman!' he declared. 'Or rather the old one come again. She was a rare pretty bird when we first met. Now she's looking trim as a bluebell again.'

'I'm very pleased for you,' Sister Joan said warmly.

There was no point in reminding him that his wife had taken the 'cure' before and lapsed after a shorter or longer time into her drinking. Padraic was devoted to his 'pretty bird' and fiercely protective of her reputation, though her alcoholism meant that he was forced to carry on his scrap-metal business and rear his twin daughters practically singlehanded. Yet his caravan was always clean, his little girls neat and polite. She would remind herself that appearances weren't always what they seemed the next time she saw a gaudy car with the side hanging off and the sweetish scent of 'grass' drifting in heavy white clouds through the windows.

'I'll be over with some nice fresh trout tomorrow, Sister,' he said, standing back.

'Sister Perpetua will be over the moon. Thanks, Padraic.' She clicked her tongue and let Lilith bound ahead.

There was no sign of the car outside the schoolhouse. Sister Joan drew rein and dismounted. She had better start thinking of the place as the hermitage now, she reflected. It was entirely wrong of her, of course, but her spell as teacher there had caused her to regard the building with a somewhat jealous air. It had been a place where for a few hours every day she had been in charge of her own space, free from the insistent sound of the bell that divided her days into segments of prayer and work, free to listen to the chatter of young children whose minds had not yet been shaped and confined in conventional patterns.

From now on the place would be barred, she supposed. Hermits weren't noted for being good company. On impulse she pushed at the door and found it unlocked. Father Stephens had driven off without securing it properly.

Inside was the square hallway with doors to left and right. The tiled cloakroom with its two chemical toilets had been scrubbed and swept, a basin and jug placed on a trestle table. There were pots and pans hanging where coats had once been draped. Clearly the cloakroom had become the kitchen with adjoining toilets. Presumably hermits weren't too fussy.

She pushed open the right-hand door which led into the larger room where she had held her classes. The chairs and flat-topped desks had been ranged against one wall, and a camp-bed placed where her own desk had been.

The table where her pupils had sat drawing pictures or eating their sandwiches on wet days had been scrubbed clean and placed near the chair on which she had sat.

Father Stephens had obviously been working hard to make the place welcoming, even to the extent of placing a china jug on the table with a flower in it. A perfect red rose with its petals beginning to uncurl slowly in the warmth of the day.

Sister Joan stared at it for a moment, and then she was backing out on to the moor again, her palms slippery as she seized Lilith's rein, scrambled to the saddle, and set off at full gallop for the convent grounds.

Four

'Do you have to ride like Paul Revere or is the town on fire?' Sister Perpetua enquired as Sister Joan drew rein in the yard.

'It's a lovely morning for a gallop,' Sister Joan said, somewhat weakly.

'When you've finished playing cowboys,' Sister Perpetua said, 'Magdalen's waiting for you to show her round the grounds. Bernadette went off to give Sister Martha a hand with the weeding, but Magdalen said she'd wait until you returned.'

Clearly the request had irritated her. Sister Joan led Lilith into her stall and unsaddled her. Until the pony had been rubbed down and watered Magdalen Cole would have to wait.

'You're back, Sister Joan.' Magdalen's soft voice had sounded from the yard.

'I'll be with you in a moment.' She went on with her task, giving herself a little time in which to work out what questions to ask the visitor.

When she emerged from the stable Magdalen was standing on the cobbles, the sunlight turning her eyes to silver, a strand of pale coppery hair escaping from beneath her white scarf.

'Come along then!' She spoke briskly. 'We'll take a walk round the grounds.'

'Did you get it?' Magdalen asked the question eagerly as they went beneath the stone arch towards the low wall of the enclosure gardens.

'Yes. A policeman friend gave me one so you may have

your money back.' She dug in her pocket for alarm and notes.

'You told the police?' Magdalen looked anxious.

'Not about you.' Sister Joan had paused, still holding the little box. 'I'll take the knife, please,' she said firmly.

'One needs protection these days,' Magdalen said uneasily.

'Not to the extent of carrying illegal weapons. Look, if you're allowed to walk around with a flick knife then we'll have to even up things and give one to Bernadette too and that would be ridiculous.'

'Yes it would,' Magdalen said. 'Bernadette doesn't care about protecting her virtue. To tell you the truth, Sister, I don't think she's a virgin.'

'You can tell by looking, can you?' For the life of her she couldn't stop distaste from colouring her voice. 'The knife, please?'

'Here.' Magdalen handed it over reluctantly. 'May I have the alarm?'

'Of course, but don't test it out because it makes a dreadful screaming noise. You strap it to your wrist and press the red spot but you won't be needing it here.'

'What about the knife?'

'That isn't your concern.' Sister Joan wondered what on earth she was going to do with it. 'If you've reason to be afraid wouldn't it be a good idea to tell someone about it? Two heads are better than one, you know.'

'Oh, I'll be safe here,' Magdalen said.

Opening the wicker gate that led into the enclosure garden, Sister Joan thought of the dark figure swirling past her down the stairs, the long pencil of torchlight moving outside the windows of the chapel corridor, the red rose on the step, the red rose in the china jug. Mentioning these things might panic the girl completely so for the moment she'd let it lie. Instead she waved to the two figures toiling at the far end of the vegetable garden and began to point out the various features of the enclosure, the rows of vegetables, the fruit bushes and trees.

'Sister Martha has the green fingers here,' she said. 'We eat most of the produce ourselves and Sister Perpetua takes the rest to market and makes a small profit on it there for us. Are you interested in gardening?'

So far the other had revealed nothing of her likes and dislikes, though she had hinted fairly broadly that she hadn't much time for her fellow guest. There had been the nasty little spike of malice in her comment.

'I don't know anything about gardening,' Magdalen said.

'This leads across to the old tennis courts.' Sister Joan unlatched the further gate and allowed the other to precede her. 'I'm afraid that the courts haven't been used for years though we could utilize them in some way. The postulancy is over there. Did you see the novice mistress, Sister Hilaria, with her charges? Both of them enter the novitiate proper after Sister Teresa is professed but they'll very probably go on sleeping in the postulancy because there aren't so many cells in the main house. You see we're given loads of time in which to make absolutely sure that we do have a vocation.'

'I won't need any time,' Madgalen said. 'I'm going to join the Order.'

'Well, that's something for you to discuss with Mother Dorothy,' Sister Joan said, wondering if the other thought that walking into the religious life was as easy as walking in to sign on the dole. 'We have to be sure that you stood a chance of fitting into our particular community or not. It takes a minimum of four years before one can be professed. How do your family feel about it? – your becoming a nun, I mean.'

'My parents are dead,' Madgalen said. 'I've no other relatives.'

'Surely that's unusual?' Sister Joan said in surprise.

'They were both the only children of only children.' Magdalen sounded dismissive.

'So you've no aunts, uncles, cousins?'

'Nobody at all,' Magdalen said serenely. 'I'll be able to provide a dowry though for the convent. I understand one needs a dowry.'

'Whatever one can afford,' Sister Joan said. 'Sometimes in cases of extreme poverty the rule is waived, of course. A vocation certainly doesn't depend on one's ability to pay for it. Here comes Alice, hunting rabbits as usual. She hasn't managed to catch one yet but she lives in hope.'

She whistled and Alice came bounding out of the shrubbery, flinging herself upon them with excited little yaps.

'The enclosure doesn't seem to be very securely guarded,' Magdalen said.

'A convent is a spiritual centre. There's such a thing as divine protection too, you know. I wish you would tell me what's really troubling you.'

She had gone too far too fast. Magdalen turned abruptly, saying, 'Hadn't we better get back? You must have chores to do. I'm very willing to help. I don't mind domestic work at all.'

'Was that what you did – what you do?' Sister Joan hurried to catch her up.

'Not as a job, no. I can cook and clean though. Thank you for the tour of the grounds. They're larger than I realized. I'll go and wash my hands.'

There was no point in labouring the matter or trying to force a confidence where no trust existed. Sister Joan fixed her mind on her chores and set the other problems aside. She doubted if anything had been taken from the library or the storeroom but when she had a spare moment she'd slip up and have a quick look round.

The day trundled on peacefully. Magdalen, to give her credit, seemed to have fitted readily into the routine. Slim and silent, she ate her lunch, helped with the washing-up, wound wool for Sister Mary Concepta who was beginning on a scarf, sat meekly on a stool in the parlour while Mother Dorothy led a discussion on the disciplines required in the religious life.

'Some fit very easily into community life. Others have to be tempered in the flame that they may become shining steel,' Mother Dorothy was reading.

And some, like me, have to be knocked in shape over and over again, Sister Joan thought, catching her superior's eye as she rose and quietly slipped from the room.

In the library Sister David was bent over a catalogue of new classical translations. One of Sister David's greatest pleasures was to pick out the books that she firmly intended to buy for the library when she had enough money. That she never would have sufficient money and that few were as crazy about the ancient tongues as she was had never occurred to her. She looked up as Sister Joan arrived on the landing, pushing her spectacles further up her tip-tilted nose as she breathed, 'Would you believe it, Sister? St Augustine's *Confessions* have been translated into Mandarin. That would be quite an acquisition to the library, don't you think?'

'I didn't know you read Mandarin, Sister David!' Sister Joan said, startled.

'Oh, I don't, but to have the volume here – it would be most interesting, don't you think?'

'How much does it cost?'

'Forty-five pounds,' Sister David said with regret. 'It's printed on silk paper with illuminated capital letters. That makes it quite a bargain at the price. However, as you say – did you come to borrow a book, Sister?'

'Just to have a poke around in the storeroom.'

Sister David was the least inquisitive person in the world despite her eager nose. Poking about in storerooms amid piles of ancient newspapers and boxes crammed with unidentifiable rubbish would have seemed to her a splendid way of passing the time.

'They have a new translation of Virgil too,' she said, her eyes feasting on the catalogue again.

'If ever I inherit a fortune,' Sister Joan said, 'I'll give you enough money to restock the library.'

'Oh, that's very generous of you, Sister.' Sister David beamed as if dream had become fact. 'That would be wonderful.'

Sister Joan smiled as she went out again. For some people

the thought of the almost impossible gave as much joy as the actual. She wished she were more like that herself.

There were footsteps in the dust on the storeroom floor, but they were smudged and blurred and might even have been her own. She had already spent a year sorting through the stacks of old newspapers here with the intention of eventually compiling a scrapbook on the history of the district, but her spare time was limited and not only did the labour go slowly but she frequently found herself absorbed in some old newspaper account that had nothing to do with the scrapbook.

The intruder had walked here, paced back and forth, perhaps trying to decide what next to do. She breathed a prayer of thankfulness for the fact that he had gone out into the grounds and not turned towards the inner door which she had left unbolted as she crept up the spiral stairs.

'Did you have a nice poke round, Sister?' Sister David had laid aside the catalogue and was carefully re-covering an old paperback.

'And got exceedingly dusty. I'll rinse my hands before I go down again.'

'Fine.' Sister David put her head down and regarded her work critically.

The washroom and toilet were handy for anyone working in the library. Sister Joan snapped on the light, took a step towards the sink, and let out an exclamation of dismay.

'What's wrong, Sister? Have you hurt yourself?' Sister David came flustering in.

'There's a red rose in the sink,' Sister Joan said.

'Yes, I know. I put it there so it wouldn't wilt before I put it on the altar,' Sister David said calmly.

'You put it there?'

'It was on the desk in the library. I thought it would look better on the altar but I had some tasks to finish here so I ran some water into the sink and propped it there. You didn't prick yourself, did you? I didn't realize there were any thorns on the stem.'

'They've been stripped off.'

'That's all right then.' Placid and incurious, Sister David reached for the glue brush again.

'I'll – put it in the vase on the Lady-altar,' Sister Joan said, going back to pick it up.

It was as perfect a shape, as deep a crimson as the other two. She carried it with care, its tip dripping, down the stairs and thrust it with the first one amid the catkins.

The deep scarlet was almost concealed among the feathery catkins. It was better so, she thought grimly. The intruder had left the roses for someone to find. Most probably Magdalen. Someone wanted Magdalen to find out that he had been here; someone wanted her to be afraid. Perhaps after all she had good reason to carry a knife.

She genuflected to the altar and went back into the hall. The discussion was just winding to a close. Mother Dorothy expected her nuns to attend at least two of her lecture sessions a week, those who were absent from any writing up their own spiritual diaries or meditating in the chapel.

'Sister Joan, a moment of your time, if you please.'

She had turned back from the door of her parlour as those who had been at the discussion filed out, Magdalen among them.

'Yes, Reverend Mother?'

'I know you've already been out on Lilith today, so you'd better take the car,' Mother Dorothy said without preamble. 'It might be more convenient anyway as you'll be carrying supplies.'

'Supplies, Mother?' Sister Joan thrust roses and midnight intruders out of her head and looked attentive.

'I intend to give the news to the community at suppertime this evening,' Mother Dorothy said. 'I have rented out the schoolhouse.'

'To a hermit. Yes, I saw Father Stephens this morning.'

'And hermits do need to eat,' Mother Dorothy said. 'Father Malone and Father Stephens will have done their best to make the place habitable and Sister Jerome will have sent up some food, I'm sure, but a little more never hurt. Will you take the supplies down? Sister Perpetua got them ready after I informed her of his impending arrival.'

'Yes, of course, Mother Dorothy.'

It would be good to have a short drive out on this mild afternoon, she thought, as she went towards the kitchen. When there were problems to be solved then having some practical task helped get things into proportion again.

'You've heard the news then?' Sister Perpetua was packing a large box. 'Hermits are a rare breed these days. Well, the rent will be useful, I daresay. I'll carry it to the car, Sister. You'd most likely drop it and break the eggs.'

The car boot sagged slightly as the box was bestowed within. Sister Joan shot the vehicle an apprehensive look.

'Don't say it, Sister.' Sister Perpetua closed the boot and stood back. 'Drive slowly for heaven's sake and don't worry about supper. I'll cook it tonight.'

'I'll be back in lots of time for supper,' Sister Joan protested.

'Well, I'll save you some if you're not. Drive carefully now.'

What she was too kindly to say, Sister Joan thought, getting behind the wheel was that a meal Sister Joan hadn't cooked would be a welcome treat for the rest of the community. She snapped her seatbelt securely, waved her hand and drove out of the yard.

The car groaned and wheezed alarmingly as she guided it over the rough track. It was time they had a new car but where the money would come from was another question. Perhaps something could be saved out of the money Magdalen had paid for her visit or part of the hermit's rent could be set aside.

Away on the horizon a line of vehicles straggled over the rise. The new-age travellers had, it seemed, arrived. It was extremely intolerant of her but she hoped they wouldn't park too near the convent.

There was a vehicle nearer than the far horizon. With

misgivings she stared at the small van with its psychedelic markings that stood at the side of the schoolhouse.

'For heaven's sake! Squatters!'

Neglecting to lock up the building had been careless though she admitted that if someone had wanted to come in they could easily have broken a window. Switching off the engine she got out of the car and raised her voice tentatively.

'Hello there! There are supplies here for the – oh!'

Her gasp was one of pure astonishment as the tall, brown-habited figure came around the corner and stood staring at her, mouth curving into a smile of recognition.

'Brother Cuthbert!'*

The young monk with the flaming red hair haloing his tonsure uttered a delighted shout.

'Sister Joan! What a wonderful surprise! Nobody mentioned—'

'Nobody mentioned it to me either,' Sister Joan said, shaking hands cordially. 'What are you doing here? You're not the hermit?'

'Only for a year. Father Prior considered I needed a bit of a break from the monastery,' Brother Cuthbert said. 'I was getting too comfortable there, Sister. Too complacent if you know what I mean. No new challenges to test me. So I asked leave for a year's absence, somewhere I could be quite alone without any social activity.'

Sister Joan thought briefly of the island in the Scottish loch where Brother Cuthbert lived in company with his fellow religious. It hadn't struck her as a hotbed of social dissipation.

'It must be nearly two years since you came up on retreat there,' he was continuing.

'Two years this autumn. You were very helpful to me then.'

'All part of the service, Sister.' He laughed again as if the joy of living were too overwhelming to be contained in a

* See *Vow of Sanctity*

smile.

'And you've come down here to be a hermit?'

'Father Prior agreed that a change would benefit me spiritually. I'd completely forgotten that your convent was in this area. Well, this is marvellous! To arrive in a strange place and meet an old friend straight off!'

'You're supposed to be here as a hermit,' Sister Joan reminded him.

'Very true, Sister. You do well to remind me.' He looked as contrite as a large young man with a perennially cheerful expression could look. 'However I don't start being a hermit proper until tomorrow. And I've not taken any vow of silence. So how can I help you?'

'Mother Dorothy, our prioress, sent down supplies for you. They're in the boot of the car.'

'I say! That was kind. Everybody has been marvellous. I called in at the presbytery in town to get the key but the place was unlocked when I got here.'

'You met Father Malone then?'

'Father Stephens. Father Malone was making a school visit, giving a talk about the pilgrimages he took last year. With illustrated slides and photographs.'

'Which Father Malone will show you the first chance he gets.'

'That will be a real treat,' Brother Cuthbert said without irony. 'Shall I carry in the supplies, Sister?'

'Thank you.'

Sister Joan opened the boot and watched him heave up the big box. Since meeting this particular monk she had ceased to regard Cuthbert as a somewhat wimpish name for a saint.

'Come along inside, Sister,' he invited over his shoulder. 'The good fathers have taken immense trouble over the place. A shower and two toilets and a Calor gas stove to cook on, and a marvellous bunk bed – my only worry is that I shall be too comfy here. A hermit's life should be more ascetic, I feel.'

'You'll find it pretty lonely here all by yourself,' she answered.

'Then that will be a new experience for me,' he said cheerfully, setting the box down. 'I've been round congenial people all my life so it will be interesting to find out how I manage by myself. Oh, apples and pears! And spaghetti and potatoes and dried milk and tea – how much do I owe you for this, Sister?'

'It's a gift.'

'That really is kind,' Brother Cuthbert said. 'Do you fancy a cup of tea now, Sister? It's been a long drive down from Scotland. I slept in the van last night and it was quite comfortable but I'm out of practice behind a wheel.'

'That's your van?' She looked at the gaudily painted vehicle.

'Father Prior thought that it would be a good idea to have some transport. I bought that in Peebles – two hundred pounds and the engine goes beautifully. Not that I expect to use it much. Stand back, Sister, while I light the gas. No, I shall emulate the hermits of old and walk everywhere. Stride across the moors early in the morning with the breeze sweet as honey.'

'And the rain dripping down the back of your habit,' Sister Joan scolded. 'Brother Cuthbert, you're a romantic!'

'And wouldn't it be a dull, grey world if all the romance was drained out of it?' he said. 'Sit yourself down, Sister. It's a real treat to play host. Have you been keeping well since we met?'

'Very well.' Sister Joan pulled up a chair. 'And everybody up at the loch? Are they all well too?'

It would have been useless to mention individuals. Her time in Scotland had been marked by sinister and threatening events of which the young monk remained serenely unaware.

'Everything runs along peacefully,' he said, bringing in two mugs of tea. 'There we are, Sister. Now tell me – this used to be the old schoolhouse, didn't it? Father Stephens did mention it.'

'It's convent property but since the school closed down not much use has been made of it. I used to teach here myself –

the children who couldn't get easily into the state schools in town, but the local authorities laid on a bus and I was suddenly made redundant.'

'But the work you did here must have given the children a splendid start in life,' he said. 'And being redundant means you can spend more time in the enclosure. Are you still painting, Sister? That's a marvellous talent you have.'

'Not recently,' she said regretfully. 'Are you still playing the lute?'

One of the more surprising things about Brother Cuthbert was his skill on the lute. It was more than a skill, she remembered. Under different circumstances Brother Cuthbert could have taken his place on the great concert platforms of the world.

'Oh yes. The lute and I can't long be parted.'

'I'm sure that Mother Dorothy – she's our prioress – will want you to play in chapel. Would you be willing to do that?'

'I'd be very flattered to be asked, Sister. Music always draws the soul nearer to God, don't you think?'

'It depends on the music,' she said cautiously.

'Real music,' he said. 'Pure harmony and notes that are true. But I'd not wish to push myself forward.'

'You won't,' she assured him, privately resolved to do a little pushing herself. 'You'll be coming to mass at the convent, I hope?'

'Oh yes, since that will do away with the need to mingle with crowds – not that your services are not well attended, of course. I didn't mean to imply—'

'There's just the community,' Sister Joan said, amused. 'Father Malone and Father Stephens take it in turns, week and week about. Mass is at seven in the morning and we have a benediction proper twice a week at six.'

'It will be a nice walk,' he said happily.

'And I have to get back. Oh, there may be more people on the moor than you bargained for. We have an invasion of new-age travellers disporting themselves around the place. I thought one of them was squatting here when I saw your van.'

'Well, live and let live,' he said with undiminished good humour as she went out.

'I hope they don't disturb you anyway.' She turned to shake hands again.

'Nothing much disturbs me at all, Sister,' he said cheerfully. 'Is that the convent car?'

'For its sins,' she said darkly.

'I was just wondering,' Brother Cuthbert said, 'if it might not be a good idea if you used the van while I'm here. I don't know too much about cars but that one does look a trifle elderly, don't you think?'

'I couldn't agree more,' she said fervently, 'but you'll need the van yourself. I mean if you go to church in town or—'

'I intend to live as much like a hermit as possible in this modern age,' he said. 'No, Sister Joan, you take the van and leave the old boneshaker here. It'll make me feel that I'm doing something to repay you for all your kindness.'

'In that case I'll accept it as a loan,' she said gratefully. 'Thank you, Brother Cuthbert. I'll just transfer some odds and ends and then leave you in peace. When you need supplies just let Sister Perpetua or myself know. She's the infirmarian but she helps out in a variety of ways, and at the moment I'm acting lay sister.'

'Thank you, Sister. I'm hoping to grow some foodstuffs myself,' he said, looking round optimistically at the uneven turf and its patches of heather and bracken and its farther stretches of dark peat. 'I'll see you again then. God bless!'

'God bless, Brother Cuthbert!'

And God bless the van which purred into motion as sweetly as any engine she had ever heard!

Had anyone bought a van for a couple of hundred pounds, she mused, the vehicle would have broken down within ten minutes of the money changing hands, but either Brother Cuthbert had been born under a lucky star or something about his transparent honesty called out a similar quality in others. Whatever the reason she luxuriated in the well-sprung suspension and smooth gears.

Sister Perpetua had hinted strongly that it would be a favour to the rest if she didn't get back in time to cook supper.

'And who am I,' said Sister Joan aloud, veering off the track, 'to disappoint dear Sister Perpetua?'

It would do no harm to take a closer look at the invaders. The cars and caravans had stopped and as she drew nearer the sounds of dogs barking, children crying and someone playing guitar rather badly reached her ears.

There must have been about 150 of them, she reckoned, stopping to wind down the window. They merely seemed to be more. They were not all young either. She noticed several elderly men, even an elderly woman, seated on the steps of a trailer and smoking. A bored housewife escaping from mediocrity? The woman raised her head and fixed Sister Joan with a long, hard look out of dark eyes set in a handsome, haggard face. Two youths, one with a ponytail, the other a Mohican haircut, strolled up and also stared at her.

'I'm Sister Joan, from the convent.' She wound down the window. 'Are you here long?'

'A week, a day, a year. Not important,' said the Mohican in an educated drawl.

'It is to some of us,' Siser Joan said. 'I asked because some of you may be Catholics in which case—'

'I worship the goddess,' Ponytail said.

'Fine,' she retorted amiably. 'I'm not here on the business of conversion. We do have a chapel and you're welcome to visit. Mass is at seven in the morning if there are any Catholics around so you might spread the word.'

'Fine, Sister, we'll do that.' Mohican sounded bored.

'Well, as long as you know.' She caught the dark, intense gaze of the elderly woman fixed on her relentlessly and had a sudden feeling of vulnerability.

'Hey, are you really a nun?' Ponytail demanded. He probably didn't mean to sound aggressive.

'Yes. I really am.'

'Fasting and praying and all that?'

'The whole works.'

'And no sex.'

'I've been a virgin for nearly ten years,' Sister Joan said solemnly.

'Hey, you're cool, Sister!' Ponytail said. 'Right up front cool. Any time you want something you ask for me. Name's White Wind.'

'I bet it isn't,' Sister Joan said.

'Right again,' said White Wind, and laughed. 'Hey, you fancy some grass?'

'She's probably here to check on stuff like that.' The haggard woman had uncoiled herself from the steps of the trailer and lounged over.

She was a tall woman, dark hair streaked with grey, small hoops in her ears. She reminded Sister Joan of Rosa Dartle in *David Copperfield*, lacking only the scar.

'We don't plan to cause any damage,' she said. Her voice was husky and pleasant, at variance with the hungry stare. Perhaps there was more than just tobacco in her cigarette.

'I'm sure you don't,' Sister Joan said appeasingly. 'I drove over to let a few people know they'll be very welcome in our chapel for mass if they wish to come.'

'Gathering souls, Sister?' There was a slyness in the woman's smile at variance with her voice. 'You'll need a long fishing rod!'

She moved away, pulling her long shawl round herself. Under it she wore jeans and a long knitted tunic that emphasized her gaunt figure.

'Take the grass and have a good life,' White Wind said, thrusting it at her. If she accepted it that meant less for someone else. Sister Joan put the small packet in her pocket, repressed a crazy impulse to give him the flick knife in exchange, and drove off.

Mother Dorothy and Sister Perpetua were standing on the front steps, clearly enjoying the early evening cool, when she drove up and swerved to a halt. Their faces would remain in her memory for a long time.

'What,' said Mother Dorothy, when she had caught her breath, 'is that?'

'It's a van, Reverend Mother.' Sister Joan switched off the engine and sat meekly.

'We can see it's a van, girl!' Sister Perpetua said impatiently. 'Where did you get it? Good Lord, you haven't joined up with those new-age travellers we've been hearing rumours about, have you?'

'It's a loan from the hermit, Mother,' Sister Joan said. 'He drove down from Scotland in it and, as he's determined to go everywhere on his own two feet and our car has almost given up the ghost and he made the offer, I said I'd accept subject to your approval.'

'But, good heavens, child, we can't drive round the district in that!' Sister Perpetua exclaimed.

'Actually it looks rather cheerful,' Mother Dorothy said unexpectedly. 'The colours are too bright but the designs aren't actually offensive.'

'They knock your eyes out,' Sister Perpetua said. 'What sort of hermit are we harbouring?'

'An old acquaintance of mine.' Sister Joan smiled at them both. 'When I went to Scotland to spend a month at our retreat there—'

'A very peaceful month,' Sister Perpetua said wistfully.

'Brother Cuthbert is one of the monks from the monastery there. He's a very nice young man, Mother, and has chosen to spend a year in virtual seclusion away from his Order. Oh, and he plays the lute beautifully and would be happy to play at mass if you wished it.'

'And he drove down in that? He must be colour blind,' Sister Perpetua said darkly.

'Take the van round to the yard, Sister, and then make ready for chapel,' Mother Dorothy instructed.

'Yes, Mother. Sister.' Starting the engine up again she drove decorously round to the yard and parked there.

It was, she thought, a splendid van. Sister Perpetua would get used to it in time. Meanwhile she'd better get rid of the 'grass' she'd been given. She opened the glove compartment and leaned to check there was space inside. There was plenty of space. The only thing the glove compartment held was a dark red rose, wilted now from the heat of the engine, but still retaining the essence of its perfume, the thorns stripped neatly from its stem.

Five

The roses were a series of messages, meant, she guessed, for Magdalen Cole. A lover trying to lure her back from the religious life? It was the logical answer but would Magdalen be so terrified of a lover as to want to protect herself with a flick knife and carry a rape alarm? One rose had been left on the step of the chapel door, the second in the library, which linked them to the intruder. The third had been in Brother Cuthbert's van. That argued that the lover – it was reassuring to picture him as a suitor rather than an intruder – had slipped it into the glove compartment while she and Brother Cuthbert were enjoying their cup of tea in the old schoolhouse.

But why put it there? If he had wanted to bring it to Magdalen's attention it would have made more sense to put it in the convent car. What was certain was that she needed to talk to someone pretty soon.

At supper Mother Dorothy waved aside the reader and beckoned her.

'Sister Joan, instead of the usual extract from a book, perhaps you would tell the community something of the hermit?' she invited.

'There really isn't very much to tell.' Sister Joan obediently took Sister Katharine's place at the lectern. 'The year before last, as most of you know, I went up to our retreat in Scotland for a month. The retreat is built into the side of a cliff overlooking the loch and in the loch is an island where monks have lived since the days of the Saxons. Brother Cuthbert was deputed to give me any help that I required and he was very helpful. Nothing was ever too much trouble for him. I understand that he wished to spend a year living away from his community in order to follow more closely in the footsteps of the old holy men, though he would be the last person to describe himself as worthy of them. He is young and strong and he plays the lute like an angel. He will be coming here for mass and to benediction but for the rest, though he's taken no vow of silence, he intends to depend on his own resources as much as possible.'

'Will he be offering mass himself, Sister Joan?' Sister Gabrielle asked.

'He isn't an ordained monk,' Sister Joan said.

'Thank you, Sister. You may sit down.' Mother Dorothy rapped her spoon. 'We will get on with our supper in silence if you please. It would be useful to think about the spiritual benefits the presence of a hermit might bring to our community. Next week Sister David will be reading for us for supper. We shall be hearing the story of Saint Bernadette.'

She smiled in the direction of Bernadette Fawkes who smiled back cheerfully.

'I didn't know Saint Bernadette was a hermit,' she remarked.

'She lived a recollected life, my dear, which amounts to the same thing,' Mother Dorothy said. 'Sister David, you might want to prepare a little talk on hermits proper? Saint Peter of Alcantara springs to mind.'

'Yes, Mother.' Sister David looked pleased at the prospect of doing anything vaguely connected with research.

The rose had been stuck in a jug of water behind a large packet of washing-up liquid. When Magdalen came to help she'd see the bloom and Sister Joan was interested to see her reaction.

'The meal is ended. Go in peace.' Mother Dorothy blessed them as they rose and filed into recreation, Sister Hilaria gathering up her charges for the walk over to the postulancy where Sister Teresa would be eating her solitary meal.

She stacked the dishes, hearing Sister Gabrielle say behind her as she leaned on Bernadette's arm for the short trip into recreation, 'So we've got a resident hermit in a manner of speaking? If you ask me this place is becoming as crowded as Piccadilly Circus on a Saturday night!'

'Doesn't Sister Gabrielle like people coming here?' Magdalen arrived in the kitchen on Sister Joan's heels.

'Sister Gabrielle adores lots of company,' Sister Joan said. 'She also loves to grumble. She regards it as a privilege of old age.'

Magdalen was sorting out cutlery, her scarfed head bent. The look on her face was closed up, remote. Sister Joan wondered how it would be if that face ever flashed into life.

'She and Sister Mary Concepta are very old, aren't they?' she said.

'Both in their eighties but very valuable in the community,' Sister Joan said.

'Are they?' Magdalen's eyebrows had risen slightly.

'They are both experienced,' Sister Joan explained. 'Sister Gabrielle gives the best advice you could hope to have if you have a problem, and Sister Mary Concepta is a marvellous example of someone who doesn't allow physical pain to sour her nature. And looking after them gives us all a chance to exercise charity. We'll be the poorer when they go.'

'I'm sure.' Magdalen had picked up the box of washing powder and was staring at the rose.

There was nothing in her face to hint at any feelings she might have had and, after a moment, she said, her tone one of mild interest, 'Surely it's early for roses?'

'Very early for hothouse varieties,' Sister Joan said. 'I found that one.'

'The petals are drooping,' Magdalen said and went over to the sink to run hot water into it. 'Shall I wash up tonight, Sister?'

So much for hoping she would be startled into a confidence! Sister Joan picked up the drying-cloth and applied herself silently to her chores.

The last practical tasks of the evening always fell to the lay sister who was the last to retire and the first to rise. Alice had to be let out for her final scurry round, Lilith in her stall to be provided with feed in case she fancied a midnight snack, doors and windows to be checked and where necessary locked, the lights that were left burning to be turned low. Coming into the chapel wing she hesitated before the door leading to the outside. She had resolved to bolt it but there was no access to the main building and to close the chapel door against an intruder who left red roses seemed undue caution, quite apart from being contrary to Mother Dorothy's wishes.

She left the outer door unbolted, bolted the inner door, and went into the cell leading off the kitchen with a far from tranquil mind. What she needed to do was talk to somebody about the recent sequence of events. If she talked to Mother Dorothy or any of the sisters she might well prejudice Magdalen's chances of entry into the Order. Postulants who were pursued by lovesick young men were liable to be a nuisance. If she talked to Detective Sergeant Mill he might take action about the flick knife.

Her last conscious thought as she slid into a dreamless sleep was that she ought to be awake and worrying.

Morning brought nothing out of the ordinary at all. Looking round the chapel when she had unbolted the inner door she was relieved to see that no extra flowers had joined those already in the vases. Everything was as it had been, and with a suddenly light heart she went blithely up the main staircase, ringing the little bell, and informing the community that Christ was risen.

By the time Father Malone had arrived to offer mass the early morning sun was climbing higher up the cloudless sky. Long rays of sunlight pierced the rose window above the crucifix behind the altar and patterned Father Malone's green surplice with dancing motes of gold. On such a day it was easy to think well of the human race.

Raising her head briefly she felt eyes on her, considering, critical eyes. The short hairs at the back of her neck prickled slightly. Someone was watching her but it was impossible to tell who. Magdalen sat further along the row. Sister Joan risked a quick sideways glance and bit her lip. Magdalen's seat was empty. She must have come in a few minutes late and was now kneeling behind from where that cold intense stare originated. Sister Joan frowned, trying to concentrate on the familiar ritual but the words were sliding away from her even as the sunlight retreated and a faint pattering of rain could be heard on the roof.

As the angel of the Presence was dismissed the sound of Brother Cuthbert's lute stole into the darkening chapel. She hadn't noticed him there but Brother Cuthbert, she recalled, had a way of blending into the surroundings of a religious ceremony as if he were part of the fabric of the worship. There was a little stir of pleasure in the community and the sense of being watched and weighed was gone. By the time the last note fell softly on the air the shower of rain had ceased and the sun had come out again.

Father Malone went into the sacristy: Brother Cuthbert slung his lute across his broad back and went out, face shielded by his cowl; Mother Dorothy led the way back into the main hall, but stayed by the door, watching the others file in. As Sister Joan reached her she detained her briefly.

'Run after Brother Cutbbert and ask him if he would like to join Father Malone and the rest of us at breakfast, will you?' she murmured. 'I think he was too shy to stay behind.'

Sister Joan doubted it. Brother Cuthbert wasn't so conscious of himself as to be shy, but the errand was a welcome one. She had a sudden need to run, to shake off the unnerving sensation that had overcome her in the chapel.

Brother Cuthbert was tall with long legs and an apparently inexhaustible supply of breath. By the time she reached the front gate he was already a small figure on the moor ahead.

'Brother Cuthbert! Brother Cuthbert!' Sister Joan sped after him.

'Who—?' The young monk had turned at her shout, as she panted up. 'Sister Joan! nothing wrong, I hope?'

'Reverend Mother asks if you'd like to take breakfast with

us.' Sister Joan put her hand to her side where a stitch threatened.

'Was I expected to stay?' he asked. 'I'm very sorry, Sister. I had no idea.'

'It's entirely up to you, Brother Cuthbert!' Sister Joan let out a breath in a whoop. 'Heavens! Are you in training for a marathon or something?'

'It's a bad habit of mine to rush about everywhere. Father Prior is always telling me about it. That's very kind of your prioress but if I'm going to be a hermit then I feel I ought to start as soon as possible,' he said earnestly. 'The supplies at the schoolhouse will last me for a very long time. You have a beautiful chapel, Sister. I know one can pray anywhere but it's always nicer to have a lovely place to do it in.'

'The moor's not looking so bad this morning,' she said.

'You're absolutely right, Sister.' Brother Cuthbert beamed at her. 'The moor looks grand after the rain. One could pray here easily. Now, will you please give Mother Dorothy my regrets and apologies?'

'Yes, of course. She'll quite understand. Brother Cuthbert, did you give anyone a lift down here in your van?'

She sounded as casual as she could as she tacked on the question.

'Yes, as a matter of fact I did.' Brother Cuthbert looked surprised. 'Not all the way down but there was a young man I picked up just this side of London. He was hoping to meet up with a friend at Falmouth.'

'What was he like?'

'I got the impression his friend was a red Indian or something. His name was Julian. Julian – I don't think he gave me a surname. I mean the one I gave a lift, not the friend. He didn't talk much. Why?'

'Did he mention that his friend was called White Wind?' she asked.

'Yes. Yes, he did. That was what made me think of red Indians. I suppose they're called Native Americans now though.'

'This one,' Sister Joan said dryly, 'is of the British variety. Thank you, Brother Cuthbert.'

'I'll probably see you around, Sister.' He raised his hand, gave a cheerful wave, and strode off again, whistling.

So now she had a lead. Turning and walking back at a more sedate pace, she wondered what good it did her. Obviously Magdalen had a boyfriend who'd followed her and brought with him three expensive, hothouse roses. He'd have done better to have given her the roses openly and been frank about his feelings instead of sneaking around, leaving other people to find them.

She was late for breakfast. Father Malone drove past her as she entered the main gates, slowing for long enough to call,

'Nice young man, Sister! And doesn't he play beautifully! An illustrated talk with music might be arranged later on.'

He was past in a screech of tyres. Father Malone alternated between driving like a nervous old lady and imagining he was competing in a Grand Prix. Sister Joan sent up a hasty prayer on his behalf and went up the drive in time to see Sister Hilaria coming round from the back, a covered dish in her hands.

'Good morning, Sister Joan!' She paused, looking at her burden. 'Would you have any idea where I'm off to with this.'

'Is it Sister Teresa's breakfast?' Sister Joan guessed.

'Of course it is! I went to the kitchen to collect it for her. Not very long before she joins us again as a fully professed Sister of the Daughters of Compassion! Such lovely music this morning. A talent like that is quite rare. It quite dispersed the very strange atmosphere.'

'Strange, Sister?'

There was never any point in hurrying Sister Hilaria when she was talking. She always lost the thread of her discourse and became confused.

'Out of place,' she said now, frowning slightly. 'Didn't you feel it, Sister? It was as if something foreign, something – awkward had stolen into the harmony. The music sent it away again.'

'Yes, Sister, I know exactly what you mean,' Sister Joan said.

'I must take this to Sister Teresa. Good morning, Sister.'

The tall, heavily built novice mistress plodded off.

Something foreign, awkward, out of place. Sister Joan nodded a trifle grimly. Sister Hilaria had put her finger on the central problem without realizing it. She might forget where she was going occasionally or absentmindedly imagine it was afternoon before she'd eaten her lunch but she had an unerring instinct about other, less practical matters. If Sister Hilaria sensed discord then a discord existed.

When she went into the kitchen she found Sister Perpetua doing the dishes while Alice sat, hopefully waiting for scraps.

'Brother Cuthbert was invited to breakfast,' Sister Joan said, hurrying in. 'I was sent after him, but he preferred to go on to the school. He wants to be a real hermit while he's here, he says.'

'Nice music,' said Sister Perpetua, tossing her a drying-up cloth. 'Nice young man too, I think. Genuine. I like genuine types – oh, Magdalen went up with Sister Katharine to help with Sister Teresa's dress. She does make herself useful, I must admit.'

'But you don't like her?' Sister Joan shot the older woman a look.

'There's nothing to dislike. Sister Hilaria put her finger on something last evening. She came over to see me about something or other and said, "Ah, you're alone!" without noticing that Magdalen was here. I know! Sister Hilaria is apt to be vague but her eyesight's perfectly sound. It was as if Magdalen had simply faded out of consciousness. Very odd.'

'Aren't nuns supposed to avoid singularity?'

'Not to the extent of becoming invisible,' Sister Perpetua said, splashing water into the sink. 'Now the Bernadette child is a lively spark. Good sense of humour and no nonsense about being holy. Anyway the two of them haven't been here five minutes so we shall have to see. Pass me that coffee pot, Sister. If I know you it'll not have been cleaned out properly in a month.'

Which was Sister Perpetua's way of saying she didn't want to gossip. Sister Joan, taking her cue, got on with the chores, then put Alice on her lead and took her out to the tennis courts to do some training.

The session progressed slowly, probably because she and the dog couldn't take it too seriously. Alice had learned to come on command but she usually came anyway if she was anywhere in the vicinity in the confident expectation of a welcome and possibly a biscuit. The problem was trying to impress on her that being friendly to the whole world wasn't the mark of a trained guard dog.

'Stay! Stay, Alice!' She backed off slowly, willing the dog to remain in her alert sitting position.

'Are you training her?'

Magdalen's soft enquiry came from the top of the moss-grown steps where she stood, peering down, her eyes silvered by the sun.

'I was.' Sister Joan spoke curtly as Alice leapt up the steps, all wagging tail and licking tongue.

'I'm sorry. I didn't mean to interrupt.' Magdalen came down the steps. 'Sister Katharine and Bernadette are sorting out the linen so I came out for a walk. I don't think one should make a nuisance of oneself, do you?'

'I'm sure Bernadette wasn't making a nuisance of herself,' Sister Joan said.

'No, of course not, Sister.'

'And guests really aren't forced to help out with anything.'

'I want to be more than a guest. I want to be a Daughter of Compassion.' Magdalen spoke in a level tone which was curiously more impressive than if she had sounded emotional. Only her hands, clenched into fists, hinted at intensity.

'You haven't been here long enough to make such a big decision,' Sister Joan said as gently as she could. 'You're still very young.'

'I'm twenty-seven,' Magdalen said.

'But I thought—'

'Everybody thinks I'm about twenty so I don't bother to contradict them. Does it make it difficult – my being older? Or easier?'

'Easier probably.' Sister Joan was trying to readjust her thinking. Twenty-seven was young still but Magdalen's face was smooth as a teenager's without even the beginnings of laughter lines at eyes and mouth. She looked – untouched was the word that came into her mind. She wondered suddenly if Magdalen could possibly still be a virgin.

'So you see I am mature in my outlook,' the other said. 'I've thought for a long time about this step. You need postulants, don't you?'

'The right ones, yes. But we're not a big community. Our foundress advised that no more than fifteen nuns should comprise one convent.'

'Then you have room for three more,' Magdalen said calmly. 'That's the postulancy, isn't it?'

'When the Tarquins owned the estate it was the Dower House,' said Sister Joan, relieved to have a few facts to expound. 'The postulants sleep there and have a light breakfast there, also their own periods of recreation and study. They come to the main house for lunch and supper and to the chapel for services. They aren't supposed to talk to the professed sisters without special permission but that rule isn't too strictly kept.'

As if on cue Sister Elizabeth emerged from the front door of the postulancy, with Sister Marie at her side. They were carrying the tray and dishes that had been taken across for Sister Teresa earlier, in addition to a large wicker basket full of nuts.

'Sisters, have you met Magdalen Cole?' Sister Joan halted their progress. 'She hopes to join us.'

Sister Elizabeth smiled, ducking her head. Sister Marie promptly held out her hand, saying cordially, 'I noticed you in chapel and, of course, Reverend Mother did announce that two guests were coming.'

'I am trying to fit myself to the life of the community,' Magdalen said. She seemed to have drawn back a little.

'Well, if you do join us,' Sister Marie said with a grin, 'you'll have to wear these hideous pink smocks and huge bonnets while you're training. Mother Dorothy thinks they're cheerful! As soon as Sister Teresa is professed then Sister Elizabeth and I go into blue habits for a couple of years. I'm Sister Marie, by the way.'

'Sister.' Magdalen spoke coolly.

'Were you coming over to the postulancy, Sister Joan?' Sister Marie asked. 'We can show Magdalen round if you like. Mother Dorothy won't mind.'

'And Sister Hilaria will want to chat to her anyway. I'll send Bernadette over later,' Sister Joan said. 'I'll take the dishes back to the kitchen for you.'

Perhaps the uninhibited Marie would be able to get closer to her. Carrying the dishes she whistled to Alice who, for a wonder, obeyed and walked to heel all the way back to the kitchen. It was empty save for Sister Katharine who was taking a cup of water at the sink.

'Did Magdalen find you, Sister?' Her delicate face was anxious. 'Bernadette was helping me with the laundry and there wasn't sufficient work for two, so I suggested she go for a walk. I hope she didn't think I was being unwelcoming or anything.'

'Magdalen Cole is determined to get in here even if we barred her way with machine guns,' Sister Joan said dryly. 'Where's Bernadette?'

'Talking to the old ladies. She's very amusing,' Sister Katharine said, adding hastily, 'Magdalen seems very devoted to the idea of the religious life.'

Sister Katharine who would have been torn in pieces before she said anything nasty about another person sounded slightly constrained.

'Devotion to an ideal is a bit different from living out the actual thing as you and I both know,' Sister Joan remarked.

'Well, it's a big step to take, and she's still very young,'

Sister Katharine said.

'Twenty-seven.'

'Really? She looks almost like a schoolgirl,' Sister Katharine said in surprise.

'Untouched,' Sister Joan said thoughtfully.

She wished that she could tell Sister Katharine about the flick knife and the rape alarm, the feeling of being watched in the chapel, the three red roses – but Sister Katharine was too unworldly to give any advice.

And I, she thought as the other went out again, am quite definitely worldly. Sometimes I wonder if it's a bad thing or a good thing.

'Sister Joan, are you doing anything in particular or merely idling your time away?' Sister Perpetua enquired, coming in.

'Idling my time away,' Sister Joan said promptly.

'You're to take Alice down to the police station.'

'Why? What has she done?' Sister Joan flushed with indignation. 'Mother Dorothy said that she could stay and she's getting on with her training very well.'

'Detective Sergeant Mill telephoned and offered to take Alice on a two-week course to give her the basic training she needs as a guard dog,' Sister Perpetua said. 'He will pay for it himself which is most generous, and will be of immense benefit to Alice. You're to take her down and hand her over – or are you going to argue?'

'No, of course not, Sister. I misunderstood, that's all,' Sister Joan said. 'It's very kind of Detective Sergeant Mill to pay for the course. Shall I take her now?'

'You're to get yourself a salad sandwich and a cup of tea in town, then call on Brother Cuthbert on the way back and ask him if he would be willing to play his lute at Sister Teresa's final profession. The community will have to make do with my soup today.' Sister Perpetua grinned mischievously.

'I'll take her in the van,' Sister Joan said.

'About the van.' Sister Perpetua coughed. 'Provided Brother Cuthbert agrees, since in actual fact it belongs to his community, Mother Dorothy feels that it might be a happy idea if you were to repaint it with more suitable designs. You can do it in your spare time.'

'Yes, Sister.'

Scooping up Alice Sister Joan wondered how she was expected to stretch twenty-four hours into twenty-five.

Fortunately Alice regarded a ride in the van as something new, delightful and utterly exciting. She pranced about, sniffing happily, then settled down in the passenger seat, her feathery tail curled round her plump body.

Sister Joan fastened her seatbelt, put the van into gear, and drove out of the yard, feeling again the pleasure of driving a decent engine. And repainting it with her own designs potentially a good idea too.

Near the main gates she slowed down to wave to Sister Hilaria who stood with her eyes fixed dreamily on the sky. The two postulants were evidently still showing the guest round their quarters, Sister Marie chattering her head off, Sister Elizabeth seeing to Magdalen's comfort. They were both nice girls, she thought. It would be a pleasure to have them in the novitiate.

There was no sign of Brother Cuthbert as she drove past the schoolhouse. Either he was within meditating or had gone for a walk across the moor. On the further horizon the ramshackle cavalcade of the new-age travellers was still stretched out over the hill. So far they had caused no trouble that she was aware of, but the gypsies might have a different tale to tell.

The bright van attracted several turned heads as she steered it up the main street and into the station yard. Detective Sergeant Mill broke off his conversation with a uniformed constable on the steps and came to open the door for her.

'Good Lord, Sister! Couldn't you find anything more conspicuous?' he enquired with a grin, lifting Alice down and setting her on the ground hastily as she proceeded to wet herself.

'It is rather snazzy, isn't it?' Sister Joan grinned back, pleased to see that his dark mood had apparently dissipated. 'We borrowed it from Brother Cuthbert.'

'Brother Cuthbert being—?'

'A young monk from a community up in the Highlands. I met him when I went up there on retreat. We've rented him the schoolhouse for a year so that he can live as a hermit there. Well, as much like a hermit as modern life permits. I thought you'd have known.'

'We've been too busy keeping an eye on the new-age travellers to pay heed to a hermit or two. Constable Petrie is taking the dog to the training centre and he'll call in to keep an eye on her from time to time.'

'She's going to fret terribly,' Sister Joan said.

'For about five minutes. We're not sending her to approved school, you know,' he said, amused. 'In a fortnight she'll be back – not a fully trained guard dog, but at least inclined to listen to orders. Petrie! The dog's here.'

Constable Petrie loped up, looking with his boyishly pink cheeks rather like a large puppy himself.

'Her name is Alice,' Sister Joan reminded him sternly.

'Hi, Alice.' Constable Petrie took hold of the lead. 'Are you going to come with me?'

Not only was Alice willing to go with him but she didn't even look round as she trotted off happily.

'Have you time for a cup of tea, Sister?' Detective Sergeant Mill was looking at her.

'Yes. Yes, I have,' she said. 'There is something I wanted to talk about. I need some advice and you're the only person who can give it to me, I think.'

'Come on into the office, Sister. Don't worry about Alice. She'll be fine.' He held open the door, looking pleased at her request. Was that one reason why he and his wife had split up? Because she had found a way to solve her problems without involving her husband who was up to his eyes in his job?

'So! How can I help you?' He motioned her to a chair and then sat down himself, stretching long legs beneath the desk.

'If I were to give you a couple of facts,' she said cautiously, 'would you be bound to make an official report on them?'

'Not unless you'd broken the law.'

'Well, I haven't.' She considered for a moment, then brought out the flick knife and laid it on the desk.

'Where the devil did you get this?' he demanded.

'It – came into my possession,' Sister Joan said. 'Can you get rid of it for me?'

'You're not able to tell me how you got it?'

'Not without breaking a confidence, Detective Sergeant. I'd be unwilling to do that.'

'Well, I can certainly dispose of it,' he said frowningly. 'I would prefer to – excuse me.'

At his elbow the telephone rang sharply. He picked it up, gave his name, and listened for a moment before saying crisply,

'I'll be right there. Goodbye.'

'I'm interrupting you.' She had half risen.

'That was a call from Mother Dorothy,' he said shortly. 'One of the nuns has been attacked. Will you follow me back to the convent in your van?'

'Yes, of course. Did Mother Dorothy say who—?'

'Only that it was a serious attack. Come on, Sister.'

Pausing only to slip the knife into a drawer, he opened the door and waited with obvious impatience for her to precede him.

Six

'Good of you to come so promptly, Detective Sergeant Mill.'
Mother Dorothy shook hands briskly and led the way across
the hall into her parlour. 'Sister Marie is in the dispensary
with Sister Perpetua — she's not as badly hurt as we first
feared but clearly shocked and upset as we all are. Please sit
down. Sister Joan, you may stay.'

Sister Joan, who had followed the police car in the van,
chose a stool at a little distance.

'Can you tell me what happened, Reverend Mother?'
Detective Sergeant Mill had on his brisk, official face.

'Sister Marie will tell you herself in a few moments. I was
in here when Sister Perpetua came to tell me that Sister Marie
— she is one of our postulants — had been attacked in the
grounds. I went at once to see for myself and then rang you.'

'Where precisely was she attacked?' he asked.

'In the garden. To be more precise on the rough grass
above the steps leading down to the old tennis courts. You'll
recall the postulancy where Sister Hilaria and her charges
sleep is at the far side of the courts.'

'Have you called a doctor?'

'Sister Perpetua, our infirmarian, had a look at her and
decided it wasn't necessary. She has minor cuts and abrasions
to her hands and is obviously distressed but she is adamant
that she doesn't want any fuss. Here they are now.'

Sister Marie, her usually rosy cheeks pale, limped in,
supported by Sister Perpetua.

'Detective Sergeant Mill, nice to see you again,' the latter said cordially. 'Sister Marie is quite ready to answer any questions you have.'

'How bad are the injuries, Sister Perpetua?' He sounded concerned, gentle.

'I fell down the steps as I was getting away,' Sister Marie said. She had taken off the concealing pink bonnet and had a white coif wrapped round her head. It gave her a mysterious, medieval look.

'She twisted an ankle and the palms of her hands are badly scraped,' Sister Perpetua said. 'Mother Dorothy, I don't believe it's necessary to call a doctor out but I do think she ought to go to Out Patients for a tetanus jab.'

'Sister Joan can run her down to the clinic as soon as Sister has finished answering questions,' Mother Dorothy said.

'Can you tell me exactly what happened, Sister Marie?' He looked at her.

'We were showing one of our visitors, Miss Cole, round the postulancy,' Sister Marie said. 'Sister Hilaria asked if we would like a cup of mint tea before we came over to the main house for lunch. I remembered seeing some wild mint in the shrubbery so I offered to go and pick some. At the head of the steps that lead down into the old tennis courts. I knelt down to gather the mint when I heard something – someone behind me in the shrubbery. I stood up and started to turn round and then someone grabbed my shoulder. I pulled away, skidded on a loose stone and fell. I must've put out my hands to save myself and I landed in a heap at the foot of the steps.'

She glanced wincingly at her bandaged hands.

'Did you see who grabbed you?' Detective Sergeant Mill asked.

'No.' Sister Marie shook her head. 'I was dazed for a moment after I fell, and by the time I got to my feet whoever it was had gone. I did get the impression that it was a man but that was just an impression.'

'He didn't follow you down the steps? Didn't check on whether or not you were badly hurt?'

She shook her head again.

'I don't think so – no, I'm sure he didn't. I scrambled to my feet – my ankle was hurting and the palms of my hands were stinging – and made my way as fast as I could back to the postulancy. Sister Hilaria came with us over to the main house but nobody had seen anything. They'd been in the little kitchen at the back of the postulancy boiling water for the tea.'

'You mentioned that you had visitors?' He slightly stressed the plural.

'Bernadette Fawkes and Magdalen Cole,' Mother Dorothy said. 'Both of them wrote to me expressing an interest in the Order, and are staying with us for a short period in order to learn more about it.'

'And nobody at the main house noticed anything?' He looked from one face to the next.

'Nobody, Detective Sergeant Mill,' she replied. 'I was here with Sister David going over some accounts; Sister Perpetua was in the infirmary with Sister Gabrielle and Sister Mary Concepta; Sister Martha and Sister Katharine had just completed their separate chores and gone into the chapel with Bernadette to pray together. Oh, and Sister Teresa is still in seclusion at the postulancy in preparation for her final profession. None of them saw anything at all, but if you wish to see them—?'

'That won't be necessary, Reverend Mother.' He was rising. 'It's fairly obvious that a trespasser isn't going to march boldly up the main driveway. Sisters, I can run you down to the clinic myself and send you back in a police car if you like. It might be more comfortable than the van for Sister Marie.'

'That's very kind of you, but since we have our own transport it would be a pity not to use it,' Mother Dorothy said, also rising. 'Sister Joan, when Sister Marie has had her injection may I suggest you stay in town for a cup of tea and a salad sandwich? Lunch here will be long over by the time you get back.'

'Yes, Mother Dorothy. Come on, Sister.' Sister Joan helped

the postulant to her feet, relieved to see that some of the colour had returned to her cheeks.

'I'll have a look around the shrubbery and the tennis courts if I may before I go,' Detective Sergeant Mill said.

'Yes, of course, and I hope you don't feel I called you out for nothing,' she said.

'Any incident of this type ought to be reported immediately,' he assured her. 'I can send a constable up to keep an eye on things if you wish but we are somewhat short in the manpower department as usual.'

'I will advise the sisters to take precautions and not wander in the grounds alone,' she allowed. 'There's no need to send anyone over. This is a convent after all, not a fortress.'

'As you wish. Good day, Sisters.'

He went out, striding towards the side path as Sister Joan settled Sister Marie in the van's passenger seat.

'I'll drive carefully,' she said as she climbed behind the wheel. 'You're looking better already but a tetanus shot is a wise precaution.'

'I really wasn't much hurt,' Sister Marie said. 'Honestly, I feel a bit of a fraud for making such a fuss, but it did give me a shock.'

'I'd have screamed my head off,' Sister Joan said.

'It happened too fast for me to scream,' Sister Marie told her. 'My throat just closed up. That was the frightening part of it.'

'I can imagine.' Sister Joan drove as steadily as the undulating track allowed towards the town.

Sister Marie had closed her eyes and leaned her head against the seat rest. The incident had probably upset her more than she liked to admit.

At the clinic she was startled to find two nurses waiting at the door to shepherd them into the surgery.

'Mother Dorothy from the convent just telephoned us to expect you,' one of the nurses said cordially. 'We'll whisk you in to save waiting.'

Sister Joan settled herself in the waiting-room and ignored

the temptation of a shiny magazine in favour of a quick and silent rosary, her fingers sliding over the beads and half hidden in the folds of her grey habit. When Sister Marie limped out, having been provided with a rubber-tipped stick, the nurse with her spoke cheerfully.

'Not too much damage. The tetanus jab will take care of any infection. Your Sister Perpetua did a good job of the bandaging. We could do with her down here! Go and have something to eat now, Sister, and keep off that foot for a couple of days.'

'There's a café just round the corner, if you can walk that far,' Sister Joan began.

'I'll be fine,' Sister Marie said. 'Honestly, Sister, it's nothing at all really.' Nothing it might be but she was breathing hard by the time they had rounded the corner and entered the café, gay with its red and white checked tablecloths and vase of plastic flowers.

'A pot of tea for two and two cheese and tomato sandwiches,' Sister Joan smiled at the girl who came from the back to serve them. 'Oh, and a glass of water, please. Sister Marie, did they give you any painkillers?'

'I'm to take two every six hours,' Sister Marie said.

'Take a couple now with the water and then we'll have our snack.'

'Have you had an accident, Sister? It is Sister, isn't it?'

The woman who had paused at the open door of the café came in, her shawl wrapped tightly about her gaunt person.

'A slight mishap, Miss—?' Sister Joan looked a question.

'Dacre. Sylvia Dacre. Miss, though I prefer Ms.'

'Sister Marie slipped down some steps,' Sister Joan said, censoring the details.

'I saw you coming out of the clinic. You're Sister Joan. You gave your name when you were talking to the two young men.'

'They're travelling with you?

'I give them house room.' The woman's lip curled slightly. 'I'm glad it was nothing serious,' she said abruptly and turned on her heel, striding out again.

'Odd woman!' Sister Marie gulped down her pills with a

grimace and picked up the sandwich the waitress had just set down.

'She's with the new-age travellers,' Sister Joan said. 'Eccentric, I daresay.'

'It's nearly two years since I was in town,' Sister Marie confided, biting with relish into her sandwich. 'Is it all right to chat like this? I mean, you're a professed nun and we're not supposed to talk to the professed sisters as a general rule.'

'You'll be a novice very soon,' Sister Joan reminded her, 'and this is an unusual occasion.'

'Thank goodness for that!'

'You're sure you didn't see anybody?' Sister Joan asked.

'Nobody. I never got the chance to turn round.' Sister Marie paused, the sandwich halfway to her mouth again as she said, 'Have you got any idea who it could be? I don't have any enemies I can think of but perhaps it was just a random attack?'

'Probably.' Sister Joan frowned slightly.

Random attackers didn't, of course, follow any rules but it seemed a long way to walk in the hope of catching a nun unawares.

'Well, it's a good sandwich anyway,' Sister Marie said cheerfully. 'Nearly as nice as the ones you make.'

'Didn't anyone ever tell you the Devil is father of all lies?' Sister Joan said, amused. 'My sandwiches are improving but they're not cordon bleu!'

'When I'm a novice,' Sister Marie said, 'that means I get to help out with lay duties, which is something I've always wanted to do. When I'm professed I shall volunteer as lay sister.'

'That'll be a burden off my shoulders,' Sister Joan said. 'Being a lay sister is hard, you know, having to balance so carefully the practical and the spiritual. It wasn't until I took over as lay sister that I realized we just don't appreciate them sufficiently – but I've a feeling you'll make a good one.'

'Sister Elizabeth prefers the contemplative side of religious life,' Sister Marie informed her. 'She's devoted to Sister

Hilaria – well we both are, but Elizabeth wants to be exactly like her.'

'Sister Hilarias are born and not made,' Sister Joan said, thinking of the quiet, obedient, slightly dull Sister Elizabeth who, unlike Sister Marie, would have been horrified to find herself sitting in a café drinking tea.

'Is Magdalen Cole really going to enter the religious life?' Sister Marie sipped her tea and fixed questioning eyes on her companion.

'She seems very keen on the idea, but that's something for Mother Dorothy to decide,' Sister Joan said.

'Reverend Mother is always bemoaning the lack of vocations.'

'Bemoaning' didn't sound much like Mother Dorothy's style but Sister Joan caught the general idea and nodded.

'Provided they're good strong vocations,' she said.

'Yes.' Sister Marie started on the second half of her sandwich, her face troubled.

'What do you think of Magdalen Cole?' Sister Joan asked bluntly.

Sister Marie's round face flushed and her eyes shifted slightly.

'We made her very welcome,' she evaded. 'We showed her round the postulancy and told her something of our daily routine and she was very interested, very eager to find out everything we could tell her.'

'Why don't you like her?'

Sister Marie blushed more hotly. 'We're supposed to love everybody,' she said.

'I said "like", Sister. Do you like her?'

'Not much,' Sister Marie admitted. 'I know it's dreadful of me, Sister Joan, since I've only had fleeting glimpses of her and Bernadette before today. She's very pleasant and quiet and yet she's actually quite pushy. That's how I came to lend her my bonnet.'

'You lent her your bonnet?' Sister Joan stared at her.

'With Sister Hilaria's leave, of course. Magdalen said she'd love to wear one of the postulants' bonnets for an hour just to see how it felt. She looked straight at me as she spoke and I felt obliged to offer.'

'So you weren't wearing your bonnet when you went out to pick the mint.'

'No, Magdalen lent me her white scarf and I had that on.'

'So you were wearing her scarf and she was wearing your bonnet?'

'Yes, but I don't — you think whoever jumped at me thought I was Magdalen Cole?'

'It's possible, isn't it?'

'Yes, but—' Sister Marie's brows drew together into a frown. 'How would anyone know that somebody was going out to pick mint at that particular time?'

'They didn't have to know. They were probably skulking about in the grounds, hoping to catch a glimpse of her. Then they saw the white scarf—'

'And a pink smock,' Sister Marie said. 'Magdalen Cole was wearing a grey dress. Sister Hilaria remarked she looked like one of the professed sisters.'

'Maybe she has a pink dress too,' Sister Joan said, unwilling to relinquish her theory.

'But why would anybody want to attack her personally?' Sister Marie demurred.

'You were grabbed, not actually attacked.'

'Why would anybody want to grab her then? She mentioned that she's quite alone in the world and she didn't say anything about having friends or enemies.'

'Magdalen Cole says precious little about anything at all,' Sister Joan said. 'Look, Sister, would you mind if we called at the police station before we drive back? Finish your tea. That's definitely better than mine ever is! The point is that I'd like a few words with Detective Sergeant Mill.'

'No, of course I don't mind.' Sister Marie finished her tea and dabbed her lips with the paper napkin. 'That was lovely, Sister. The throbbing in my ankle's less too. But are you sure that Magdalen is the one who was being followed?'

'No, I'm not sure, but there is another matter I ought to mention to him. I'll pay for this, Sister, and then we can get started.'

Leaving the waitress beaming at the generous tip that Sister Joan had recklessly bestowed, they made their slow way round the corner to the van.

'I'll wait inside while you go in,' Sister Marie said as they drove into the station yard.

'Give me five minutes, Sister, and then we'll be on our way,' Sister Joan promised. It was, in fact, less than a minute before she reappeared.

'Detective Sergeant Mill was called out somewhere else,' she said, climbing back into the van.

'Was it important, Sister? What you wanted to tell him?'

'I daresay it'll keep,' Sister Joan said, hoping she was right.

Magdalen Cole might not be the most charming of people but she was entitled to the same consideration as anyone else. It was time, now that there had been an actual attack on somebody, for Detective Sergeant Mill to be told that Magdalen had come to the convent expecting trouble.

Near the school she slowed and stopped as Brother Cuthbert emerged, beaming at them through the window.

'Glad to see the van's still going well,' he said. 'It was a real kindness your agreeing to take it off my hands, Sister. Walking suits me much better.'

'We were wondering if we could repaint it, Brother Cuthbert, while we're using it,' Sister Joan said.

'Do anything you like with it, Sister. Your old car's perfectly safe here.'

'I'll talk to Mother Dorothy about it. Padraic Lee from the Romany camp deals in scrap iron and might give us something for it. Oh, I'm sorry! This is Sister Marie, who is just about to enter our novitiate.'

'How are you, Sister Marie? It must be very exciting for you at this stage of your vocation,' Brother Cuthbert said.

'A bit too exciting,' Sister Joan said dryly. 'Sister Marie was attacked earlier today and might have been badly hurt if she hadn't managed to get away.'

'Attacked!' Brother Cuthbert's freckled countenance expressed the liveliest dismay. 'Who in the world would attack a holy sister?'

'Someone who was hanging about in the grounds. I don't suppose you noticed anyone going in that direction?'

'I'm afraid not, Sister.' He shook his head regretfully. 'I've been praying and meditating since this morning's mass, so I wouldn't have noticed if a legion marched past. I hope you reported it to the police?'

'And got medical attention,' Sister Joan said.

'There's such a lot of violence around these days,' Brother Cuthbert said. 'In the city one almost expects it, I suppose, but not out here. Tell you what, Sister, I'll keep an eye open for anything unusual – and the next time I take a walk I'll go in the direction of the convent. Reverend Mother won't mind if I enter the grounds?'

'No, of course not,' Sister Joan said warmly. 'She'll be happy to know there's a man keeping an eye on the premises. Oh, and she wants to know if you would be willing to play your lute at Sister Teresa's final profession. It's in just under a month.'

'Oh, that would be super!' Brother Cuthbert was beaming again. 'What an honour! You'll be wanting very happy music, of course. Tell Reverend Mother I'll be delighted.'

'That,' said Sister Marie, a quiver of laughter in her voice as they drove off, 'is a very large young man.'

'I met him up in Scotland when I went there on retreat,' Sister Joan told her. 'He has a Degree in Music and gave up a promising career as a concert performer to enter the religious life.'

'He played beautifully at mass,' Sister Marie said, catching herself in a yawn. 'Oh, I beg your pardon, Sister.'

'What you need is a couple of hours sleep and then a quiet evening with your feet up,' Sister Joan said, driving through the gates. 'I've a feeling that Mother Dorothy will wish to take a few extra precautions until this prowler is caught.'

Her surmise was correct. During the afternoon, with Sister Marie resting in the infirmary (if listening to Sister Gabrielle fulminate about the increase in crimes of violence could be called resting), Sister Joan decided to catch up with the entries in her spiritual diary. Every nun, professed or not, was expected to keep such a diary which remained private until her death. Her own diary was, she suspected, hardly the stuff to inspire those who came after, being full of shabby little faults and usually several days out of date.

'Sister Joan, can you spare me a moment?'

Mother Dorothy had opened the parlour door.

Sister Joan mentally consigned her spiritual diary into the bin marked, 'Things to do when I've got time' and followed her superior back into the wide, lovely room.

'*Dominus vobiscum.* Sit down, Sister.' Mother Dorothy resumed her seat behind her desk.

'*Et cum spiritu tuo.*' Sister Joan obeyed.

'Sister Marie seems very much better. She's a resilient young woman.' As usual Mother Dorothy came immediately to the point. 'My own view is that this was probably an isolated attempt by some sick individual to grab a female, any female. One reads about such things far too often these days. However until Alice is returned to us I think it unwise for Sister Hilaria and her charges to sleep over in the postulancy. Sister Hilaria can double up with me since my cell is large enough to hold a second bed, Sister Teresa will sleep in her old cell – you will remember she is still in strict seclusion – and Sister Marie can remain in the infirmary. Sister Elizabeth can occupy the lay cell next to your own, which leaves Magdalen without a room since she is now in Sister Teresa's old cell.'

'Magdalen Cole can take the other lay cell,' Sister Joan said promptly. 'I can bunk down in the kitchen on the old settee there for a few nights.'

'Thank you, Sister. There was nothing found in the shrubbery by the way save a few broken branches, but Alice is always burying her bones there.'

'I'm sure she won't have any bad habits when she comes back,' Sister Joan said.

'Your optimism is very touching,' Mother Dorothy said dryly. 'There is another matter on which I'd like your opinion. Magdalen Cole.'

'Yes, Reverend Mother?'

'As you know, Sister, there is a sad shortage of vocations in every Order and when Sister Marie and Sister Elizabeth enter the novitiate we shall have no postulants at all. I cannot, in conscience, hold them back any longer on that account, but the postulants represent the future of our Order. Magdalen Cole has told me that she wishes to apply immediately to enter our convent. She is devoted to the ideals for which we stand and sees no reason for delay. That is what she says and I have no reason to doubt her, but I have reservations.'

'Yes?'

'She is all things to all men,' the prioress said slowly. 'When help is needed in the kitchen there is Magdalen washing dishes; when Sister Perpetua requires something there is Magdalen on the way to fetch it; when Sister Katharine needs help with the sewing Magdalen reveals herself as a very competent needlewoman.'

'Surely it's natural she should try to please, to fit in?' Sister Joan said fairly.

'Would you agree with me that it would be best to delay my decision until a few more days have passed?'

It was most unlike Mother Dorothy to solicit for opinions. Sister Joan guessed that like herself the prioress wasn't sure what to make of the visitor.

'That seems an excellent idea,' she said aloud.

'Thank you, Sister.' Mother Dorothy nodded, signing the air with a blessing.

'Is Sister Marie all right?' Magdalen glided down the staircase as Sister Joan came into the hall with the prioress.

'Much better,' Mother Dorothy said. 'Oh, there are to be changes in the sleeping arrangements for a few days. You won't mind using the lay cell where Sister Joan sleeps?'

'I'm bunking down in the kitchen,' Sister Joan said cheerfully.

'Oh no, Sister!' Magdalen's face had flushed. 'I can bunk in the kitchen – no, I insist. I wouldn't dream of taking Sister's bed. Honestly!'

'One could put up a fourth bed in the infirmary, I suppose,' Mother Dorothy said.

'Then with your leave I'd rather sleep there,' Magdalen said quickly. 'More company!'

'Very well, if that's convenient for the others.' Mother Dorothy nodded and turned away.

'Pushy' had been the word that Sister Marie had used. Pushy in an oblique, subtle way. Magdalen had turned and was drifting away. Perhaps she was more nervous than she liked to admit, Sister Joan reflected. She wondered uneasily if she ought to have mentioned the flick knife to Mother Dorothy, but to have done so would have put paid to any hopes Magdalen entertained of entering the postulancy. No, she'd wait until she saw Detective Sergeant Mill again.

At supper word that sleeping arrangements were to be changed was greeted with a buzz of interest which Mother Dorothy instantly quelled.

'Anyone would think you had been requested to emigrate,' she said tartly. 'It is merely a temporary measure to avoid having Sister Hilaria and the postulants walk through the grounds after dark. During the day they may return there, but never alone, until this prowler is arrested. It was probably an isolated incident but one likes to be sure. For the moment you should all try not to wander alone in the grounds.'

'I can help Sister Martha in the garden,' Sister David offered.

'Thank you, Sister. Detective Sergeant Mill is of the opinion that one of the so-called new-age travellers may have trespassed in the enclosure and thought it a joke to frighten one of the sisters, and he has every confidence they'll be moving on again soon. What is it, Sister Joan?'

'I'm sorry, Reverend Mother,' Sister Joan said, 'but I forgot to mention that I spoke with Brother Cuthbert when I was on the way back from the clinic with Sister Marie. He would be honoured to play the lute at Sister Teresa's final profession. I also told him what had happened here and he was very concerned about it. He says that he'll take his walks in the convent grounds in future and keep a sharp eye open for any suspicious characters.'

'Excellent!' Mother Dorothy looked pleased. 'Shall we now get on with supper?' It was a vegetable risotto with tinned tuna mixed in, not one of her happier dishes, but it was eaten as usual with every appearance of enjoyment. Glancing down the table to where Magdalen sat, a white scarf wrapped again about her hair, she saw that the guest was also eating with a smiling face. It would have been more honest to have pushed the food about her plate, Sister Joan thought, and immediately blamed herself for being intolerant.

The truth was that she would never care much for Magdalen Cole whatever she did. That was something else to be recorded in her spiritual diary the next time she brought it up to date.

She was stacking the dishes when Magdalen came up, her eyes lowered as if she had already learned custody of them.

'If you don't need me, Sister, I would like to help bring things over from the postulancy,' she murmured. 'I haven't yet met Sister Teresa.'

'You won't be meeting her until she is fully professed,' Sister Joan said. 'She speaks only to the priest, to Mother Dorothy and to Sister Hilaria. She eats her meals alone, sits separate in chapel, takes her exercise when the rest of us are working. It would be quite impossible for you to meet her.'

'Yes,' said Magdalen softly. 'Of course I wouldn't dream of approaching her, Sister Joan. That would be an infringement of the rule.'

'You're not bound by the rule but Sister Teresa is.'

'Yes, of course.' Magdalen hesitated, then said in the same low tone, 'And the alarm you were kind enough to get for me? Do you think I ought to mention that I have one?'

'Not unless you intend telling Mother Dorothy exactly why you felt you needed it in the first place,' Sister Joan said coldly.

'Better not. Thank you, Sister.'

Magdalen took a stack of plates and drifted out with them. Staring after her, Sister Joan bit her lip. There was never anything to complain of in Magdalen's conduct. She did more in the way of chores than a visitor would be expected to do. Not once had she laughed loudly or raised her voice or broken the silence when silence was the custom. Her coppery hair was tucked away, her grey dress almost identical to the habits of those about her, and her face innocent of make-up. At the rate she was going she'd be a Living Rule before she was halfway through her postulancy.

Sister Joan picked up another pile of plates and went down to the kitchen, deciding that she'd take Lilith out for a gallop the next morning and work off some of her own ill-humour.

Nobody had gone to recreation. Bunk beds were being carried in and blankets sorted. Sister Hilaria walked across the yard, the heavily veiled Sister Teresa at her side.

'We'll go up the backstairs and get Sister settled,' the novice mistress said.

'Yes, of course, Sister.' Sister Joan was aware of Magdalen's grey gaze from the corner of the kitchen.

Sister Elizabeth came in, carrying her things, and bobbed her head in timid thanks as Sister Joan opened the door of the empty lay cell for her.

'Sister, put on the kettle again, will you?' Sister Perpetua popped her head in at the door. 'Reverend Mother ordered an extra cup of cocoa for everybody for us to drink before we go into chapel.'

Sister Joan filled the big kettle and reached up for the cocoa. From the infirmary came a burst of laughter. Sister Gabrielle was in fine form this evening, probably stimulated by Sister Marie's presence. The feeling that they were all together under one roof was a good feeling. She felt suddenly more cheerful and managed to give Magdalen a genuinely sincere smile as they started to take round the trays of brimming mugs.

It had been a long day or, at least, it seemed to have lasted several hours beyond the usual number. Sister Joan was, for almost the first time in her religious life, glad when prayers were done and she could kneel for the last blessing of the day and then begin her final rounds.

The lights were low, Alice's basket empty, a pale moon breasting the clouds. Getting wearily into bed she went through the doors she had locked or bolted in her mind. Front door, back door, door leading into the chapel wing, door from the chapel on to the side path – she must open that first thing in the morning. Her lids fluttered down and she slept.

Waking was difficult. She lay for several minutes trying to persuade herself that her watch must be wrong. Unhappily her watch was never wrong. She dragged herself into a sitting position, groped for her stockings and shoes, stood up and reached for her clothes, the chill of early morning striking her bare shoulders as she stepped out of her nightgown. By the time she had brushed her teeth, splashed cold water on her face and fixed her veil securely she was feeling more like her usual self.

Quarter to five in the morning was no rising hour for civilized people, she reflected as she went up the passage into the main hall. The rising bell was kept in the chapel. She put her hand on the bolt of the inner door and was suddenly wide awake. The previous night she had bolted the door. She knew it had been bolted. Now it was unbolted. One of the others must have risen very early to pray in the chapel. She opened the door and went down the passage to pick up the bell, raising her voice as she swung the clapper.

'Christ is risen!'

From the infirmary came an answering chorus of sleepy voices. Sister Joan wondered if Sister Marie had slept well. Her ankle had received a nasty wrench and the palms of her hands had been lacerated.

'Christ is risen!'

No sound from the lay cell where Sister Elizabeth slept. Sister Joan bit her lip. A postulant who ignored the rising bell was in for a good hard penance. She tapped gently on the door, rapped harder, opened the door a crack, and saw in the shaft of early light coming through a gap in the curtains the staring open eyes and bloodstained face of the postulant. She had been dead for hours, the blood caked and congealed, her eyes dull, staring at nothing.

Seven

Sister Joan stood rigidly, looking down. This wasn't the first violent death she had seen but that didn't make it the less horrible. Automatically the rules of commonsense came into operation, blanketing the shock. Nothing must be touched or moved. Sister Elizabeth was dead. Sister Joan broke her own rules and touched the inside of the dead girl's wrist. The skin felt cold and damp. Her open eyes held no expression at all. Sister Joan would have liked to close them, to cross the stiffening arms on the motionless breast, but she turned away, went into the kitchen again, closed the door of the lay cell softly behind her.

Mother Dorothy was already awake when she tapped on the door of her cell. Her nightcapped head was raised from the pillow, one hand reaching for her spectacles, her voice low as she said, 'Something has happened, Sister Joan?'

'Sister Elizabeth is dead, Mother.' Sister Joan spoke bluntly, aware that the prioress was one of the few completely controlled people with whom one could be blunt. 'She didn't respond to the morning salutation so I looked in on her. Someone bludgeoned her across the forehead as she slept, I think.'

There was a slight intake of breath. Mother Dorothy glanced across to the other bed where Sister Hilaria still slept.

'Rouse the rest of the community for chapel,' she instructed quietly. 'I will telephone the police and inform Father Malone what has happened as soon as he gets here. I will break the news after mass. The police will be here by then and will wish to make the usual enquiries. You are sure Sister Elizabeth is beyond help?'

'I'm certain, Mother Dorothy.'

'Very well, Sister. Continue with the salutations.'

'Christ is risen!' Sister Joan backed out of the door, whirring her rattle again.

From within Mother Dorothy's voice answered, 'Thanks be to God!'

'Thanks be to God!' Sister Hilaria had woken and was dipping to her knees.

There was comfort in following the usual routine. Sister Joan went on down the corridor, making her announcement, hearing the responses in varying stages of alertness. Sister Elizabeth's absence from chapel might be noted but nobody would comment on the fact yet. This early hour was for contemplation and worship.

She had reached the foot of the staircase when Mother Dorothy went past her, heading for the parlour. She would be telephoning the police. Sister Joan went on into the kitchen and stood uncertainly there, looking at the closed door of the lay cell. She was tempted to look in again, to see if anything out of place there had escaped her first horrified glance, but that would be for the police to decide.

'Sister Joan!' Mother Dorothy came in, her voice having regained its usual sharpness.

'Yes, Reverend Mother?'

'Did you unlock the door leading into the chapel wing?'

'It was open when I came into the hall this morning,' Sister Joan said.

'Thank you, Sister. I've rung the police and also Father Malone. He will come at once to offer mass so that the police can get on with their enquiries as quickly as possible. Go into chapel now.'

Sister Joan went across to the chapel, genuflecting, slipping into her place as if this were still an ordinary morning. The rest of the community was filing in.

When Father Malone came from the sacristy there was a

faint stir of surprise. Mass was not due to begin for nearly an hour. One or two glanced surreptitiously at the fob watches pinned to their bodices.

Father Malone looked pinched and cold. The news would have been a terrible shock, Sister Joan thought with a pang of sympathy. The priest took a fatherly interest in all the nuns but had a particular tenderness for the postulants. Further along the row Sister Hilaria knelt upright, her face calm. For the novice mistress death held no particular fear. She had achieved a quality of detachment that made the murder of one of her charges a sad but curiously remote event.

Mass began. Sister Joan concentrated with difficulty on the service, aware that she had begun to feel shaky and chilled, the usual symptoms of delayed shock. From beyond the walls she heard a car arriving, glimpsed Mother Dorothy as she rose neatly from her seat and made an unobtrusive exit.

The last blessing was given, the angel of the Presence permitted to depart. Mother Dorothy had returned, walking swiftly up the aisle and turning to face the community.

'I am sorry to have to tell you that a sad and shocking event has necessitated my calling in the police,' she said. 'Will you please return to your cells for the moment and stay there until you are called? Breakfast will be at the usual time.'

She went out, followed by Sister Hilaria. Father Malone had gone into the sacristy. Sister Joan joined the rest as they filed out. She wished that she could have looked closely at each member of the community and reached some conclusion from their faces but the rule demanded that she pace sedately, keeping her eyes lowered.

In the kitchen Sister Perpetua had begun making tea. She turned as Sister Joan came in, her expression one of extreme distaste, her usual reaction to bad news.

'There are two policemen in the lay cell. Did you know about this?' she asked, not troubling to lower her voice.

'I found her,' Sister Joan said.

'It's a bad business,' the infirmarian said. 'On the verge of her novitiate too! What harm did Sister Elizabeth ever do to anyone? You'd better have a drop of brandy in your tea, Sister. You're white as a sheet. One might've thought we'd all be safe enough in the main house! Evil gets everywhere, it seems.'

The brandy was a liberal measure. Sister Joan choked slightly as she drank the steaming liquid but the shakiness was abating. By the time the door of the lay cell opened and Detective Sergeant Mill emerged, followed by a subdued looking Constable Petrie, she felt calmer.

'Good morning, Sister Joan.' Detective Sergeant Mill greeted her soberly. 'Petrie, you'd better wait here until the surgeon and the photographer arrive. If you smile nicely at Sister Perpetua she might give you a cup of tea. Sister Joan, you found the girl?'

Sister Joan nodded.

'Then I'd better talk to you first. Mother Dorothy has put her parlour at my disposal. Bring your tea with you if you like.'

'I've finished it.' Sister Joan put down the cup and preceded him out of the room into the short corridor that brought them to the main hall.

Mother Dorothy was seated at her flat-topped desk, her head slightly bent over a typed sheet of paper. As they entered she looked up.

'I have Sister Elizabeth's details here,' she said, her tone firm and businesslike. 'She has no close relatives, I'm afraid. Her original home was in the Midlands. She is – was twenty-four years old.'

'Young to have no close family.' Detective Sergeant Mill took the typescript from her and frowned at it.

'Her parents died when she was a child and she was reared by a grandmother who died just before Sister Elizabeth entered the postulancy. She has been with us for nearly three years and was an exemplary postulant as Sister Hilaria will testify. She can't have had an enemy in the world.'

'She had one,' he said soberly. 'Sister Joan, you found her?'

'As acting lay sister it's my task to rouse the rest of the

community first thing in the morning,' Sister Joan said. 'When Sister Elizabeth didn't reply to the salutation I went into the cell and found her.'

'You didn't move anything or touch anything?'

'I felt her wrist. There was no pulse and the skin was chilly.'

'What was a postulant doing over in the main house?' he enquired.

'After the attack on Sister Marie I deemed it wise to have the entire community sleeping under one roof,' Mother Dorothy said.

'Sleeping exactly where?'

'Sister Hilaria shared my cell which is the largest one; Sister Teresa who is on the verge of making her final profession and has been staying in the postulancy took her old cell, and Sister Marie slept in the infirmary. Magdalen Cole, the young woman now visiting us, offered to sleep in the infirmary so that Sister Elizabeth could occupy the lay cell.'

Mother Dorothy had stopped suddenly, frowning.

'Are there any lights left burning in the cells at night?' Detective Sergeant Mill asked.

'Every sister has a candle to be lit in the event of an emergency,' the prioress said. 'There are dim lights left burning on the staircase and in the upper and lower corridors, and of course we have the perpetual lamp in the chapel.'

'So whoever entered the lay cell would have had only the dim glow of the light in the passage,' Detective Sergeant Mill said.

'You're suggesting that Sister Elizabeth may have been killed in mistake for someone else?'

'I'm not suggesting anything, Reverend Mother,' he said promptly. 'Right now I'm merely considering all the options.'

'Sister Marie lent Magdalen Cole her bonnet yesterday,' Sister Joan volunteered.

'When was this?' Mother Dorothy asked.

'Before Sister Marie went out into the grounds to pick

mint. She had Magdalen's white scarf over her head when the attack took place.'

'And Magdalen Cole would have been sleeping in the lay cell if the sleeping arrangements hadn't been altered?'

Mother Dorothy nodded. Her face was troubled.

'We'd better have Miss Cole in then,' Detective Sergeant Mill said. 'Is it all right with you if Sister Joan stays?'

'If you think it might help.' Mother Dorothy sounded doubtful.

'The door leading into the chapel wing was open when I got up this morning,' Sister Joan interposed. 'It's always locked after the grand silence.'

'Ever since you warned us that we ought to take more efficient security precautions,' Mother Dorothy reminded him. 'The door can be unlocked from this side, of course.'

'Neither of you unlocked it last night?' He glanced from one to the other.

'I didn't,' Mother Dorothy said, 'and I'm sure Sister Joan didn't. She reported it to me this morning.'

'Right then, we'll have a few words with Magdalen Cole. What can you tell me about her, Reverend Mother?'

'Not a great deal.' Mother Dorothy folded her hands together judicially. 'She is from London though she has no trace of an accent. Rather a quiet, reserved young woman, very devoted to the ideals of the religious life. Her priest sent a reference with her letter of application, but she comes from a large, inner-city parish so I have no idea how well he really knows her. Sister, bring Magdalen here, will you?'

It wasn't an errand she particularly relished but she went obediently, tapping on the infirmary door before putting her head round it.

The four occupants were talking, or rather Sister Gabrielle was talking while the others listened.

'—and someone has to tell us sometime exactly what – ah, Sister! Is it true that Sister Elizabeth's been murdered?'

'Oh, it can't be!' Sister Marie raised brimming eyes.

'I'm afraid she has,' Sister Joan said, knowing that

prevarication never got one anywhere with Sister Gabrielle. 'Madgalen, the detective would like a word with you.'

'With me?' Magdalen had risen, her already pale face whitening. 'I don't know one single thing about any of this!'

'He'll want to talk to everybody,' Sister Joan said. 'He has to start somewhere.'

'Ought we not to be saying the prayers for the dead?' Sister Mary Concepta said in her gentle old voice.

The two old ladies had taken the news more calmly than the younger ones. No doubt the horror of death, even of a sudden death, lost its power when one grew older.

'Father Malone will be making the arrangements for that,' Sister Joan said.

'I can't tell him anything useful,' Magdalen continued to protest as they went down the corridor and across the hall.

'Come in, Magdalen.' Mother Dorothy spoke with brisk kindliness. 'I'm afraid we have some very distressing news.'

'About Sister Elizabeth? Yes, I know.' Magdalen squeezed her hands together and looked round wildly as if she felt trapped.

'I suspect Sister Gabrielle put two and two together,' Sister Joan said.

'Yes, of course. Sit down, Magdalen. The detective sergeant wants to ask you a few questions. Sit down, Sister.'

'I don't know anything,' Magdalen repeated, sinking onto a stool next to Sister Joan.

'These are just preliminary enquiries, Miss Cole.' Detective Sergeant Mill had adopted his reassuring manner. 'As Sister Gabrielle has surmised Sister Elizabeth has been killed.'

'Killed!' Magdalen's voice was a whisper. 'She didn't just die then?'

'Unfortunately, no. Miss Cole, did you know Sister Elizabeth before you came here?'

Magdalen shook her head. She had swathed her pale hair in the inevitable white scarf.

'But you've talked to her?'

'Only briefly.' Magdalen sat up a little straighter, clearly trying to compose herself. 'We – Berndadette and I – she's the other guest here – went over to meet the two postulants yesterday and – but you know about Sister Marie being attacked. Sister Elizabeth was very quiet and scarcely said anything at all.'

'Sister Marie lent you her bonnet?'

'Only to try on for a little while,' Magdalen said anxiously. 'I hope to enter the Order here so naturally I want to know how it feels to be a postulant.'

'It takes rather more than the wearing of a bonnet,' Mother Dorothy said dryly.

'And you lent Sister Marie your scarf?' Detective Sergeant Mill sounded patient and plodding.

'Only while she went out to pick mint for some tea.'

'And was attacked,' he said.

'But not badly hurt, thank God!' Magdalen said. A trace of colour dyed her cheeks.

'And you offered to sleep in the infirmary so that Sister Elizabeth could sleep in the lay cell?'

'I'm only a lay visitor,' Magdalen said. 'I was very comfortable on the put-u-up in the corner.'

'But until last night you'd been sleeping in the lay cell?'

'It's next to the kitchen so I can lend a hand with the breakfasts,' Magdalen said earnestly. 'I want to enter into the life of the community – oh!' She broke off abruptly, her lower lip trembling.

'Miss Cole, can you think of anybody who'd wish you harm?' he asked bluntly.

The grey eyes were wide and troubled.

'I can't think of anybody who'd want to murder me,' Magdalen said.

'Did you see or hear anything unusual during the night?'

After thinking for a moment she shook her head, her eyes dropping.

'That seems to be it for the moment.' Detective Sergeant Mill nodded pleasantly.

'If there's anything at all I can do—?' Magdalen's voice

was a soft murmur.

'Would you ask Bernadette to come to the parlour?' Mother Dorothy said. 'She is our other lay visitor, Detective Sergeant Mill, so you may wish to have a few words with her next?'

'That's an excellent idea, Reverend Mother,' he said promptly.

Magdalen glided out. The detective was looking over some notes he had jotted down. A tap on the door brought Bernadette, her long braid swinging, a slightly crumpled brown skirt and sweater on.

'I went back to change,' she said slightly breathlessly. 'I haven't anything black with me but I thought one should wear something a bit mournful. Is it true? Has Sister Elizabeth really been killed?'

'I'm afraid so, Miss—?' Detetive Sergeant Mill looked a polite enquiry.

'Fawkes. Bernadette Fawkes. I haven't,' said Bernadette with a show of spirit, 'had a change of name since yesterday!'

'No, of course not. Unfortunately one has to follow the usual procedure,' he said apologetically. 'You were in the postulancy yesterday when Miss Cole borrowed Sister Marie's bonnet?'

'Yes, just before Sister Marie went out to pick some mint. I don't see what that has to do with Sister Elizabeth though.'

'And you were with Sister Elizabeth and Miss Cole when Sister Marie came back into the postulancy?'

'With her hands scratched where she fell on the gravel and limping because she'd twisted her ankle. Yes. She said someone had grabbed her from behind. I said all that.'

'Just checking, Miss Fawkes. Now! You were sleeping in one of the upstairs rooms – sorry, cells last night?'

'In my old cell,' Sister Joan volunteered. 'Now that I'm acting lay sister I sleep in the cell off the kitchen. Sister Elizabeth took the other lay cell next to it.'

'Did you hear anything unusual during the night?' Detetive Sergeant Mill asked. Bernadette shook her head.

'Not a thing,' she answered after a moment. 'I always sleep like a log anyway.'

'You come from Yorkshire?'

'From Leeds, yes. Mother Dorothy has my address.'

'You didn't meet Magdalen Cole until you arrived here?'

'Sister Joan met us both at the station. We'd travelled on the same train from London without realizing that we were coming to the same place.'

'So you actually met on the train?' He glanced up.

Bernadette shook her head again.

'No. I didn't see her on the train but it was pretty crowded anyway.'

'And you can't think of anything else to tell us?'

'Nothing that has anything to do with Sister Elizabeth being dead,' Bernadette said. 'Perhaps there's a maniac going round trying to kill nuns.'

'It might be a good idea to keep the fruits of your imagination to yourself, my dear,' Mother Dorothy said. 'Whom would you like to see next, Detective Sergeant Mill?'

'Sister Marie, if I may.' He nodded towards Bernadette.

'Shall I fetch her?' the girl asked, rising. 'She's in the infirmary.'

'She's well enough to see us? I didn't think her injuries were very severe.' He looked surprised.

'She's fine, only a trifle shaken,' Mother Dorothy reassured. 'She slept in the infirmary, that's all.'

'Very well. Thank you, Miss Fawkes.'

'That's a nice child,' Mother Dorothy said as the door closed behind Bernadette. 'You don't seriously think that she can have had anything to do with this terrible affair?'

'I've an open mind at the moment.' He tapped the tip of his pen against the notebook he was holding. 'All I'm doing now is getting down a few facts, always bearing in mind that they may not be facts. Not that people deliberately lie, but the memory can play tricks. Anyway I'll have your two guests checked out. Ah! Sister Marie, are you feeling better?'

Sister Marie, limping in, nodded doubtfully and gave her

reddened eyelids a final rub with a crumpled tissue.

'I just can't believe that anyone would want to hurt Sister Elizabeth,' she said dolefully. 'She was always so good, so quiet.'

'You slept in the infirmary last night?' Detective Sergeant Mill smiled at her encouragingly.

'Yes. There's an extra bed there for anyone who might be ill. I went straight off to sleep and never heard a thing. I took some painkillers last night so I went out like a light.'

'You're a – postulant, aren't you?'

'About to enter the novitiate,' Mother Dorothy interposed. 'As soon as Sister Teresa makes her final profession both Sister Marie and Sister Elizabeth would have joined us in the main house.'

'Leaving Sister Hilaria without any pupils?' he asked.

'If our two visitors make formal application to join the Order that lack will be remedied,' Mother Dorothy said.

'What do you think of them?' Detective Sergeant Mill asked.

His question was directed at Sister Marie who reddened and cast a glance towards her superior.

'One must give the police every assistance, Sister, so feel free to answer frankly.' Mother Dorothy spoke reassuringly.

'They both seem very nice,' Sister Marie hesitatingly. 'Bernadette Fawkes reminds me of myself, always apt to put her foot in it and say the wrong thing. The other one is – she's very quiet and devout, but somehow or other – I've only really seen her when she came over to the postulancy. She kept saying that she didn't want to be a nuisance but the upshot was that Sister Hilaria offered to make some mint tea for everybody and I lent her my bonnet without really meaning to.'

'Thank you, Sister. You've been very helpful,' Detective Sergeant Mill said cordially. 'Would you ask Sister Hilaria to come in?'

'And keep off that ankle in case it starts swelling again,' Mother Dorothy added as the girl limped from the parlour.

Sister Hilaria came in with her usual deliberate tread, planting one large foot in front of the other, her large hands folded in her sleeves, her gaze calm.

'Good morning.' She greeted the detective politely but without any sign of anxiety as if his being there was of small interest. 'Mother Dorothy, are we to arrange a requiem for poor Sister Elizabeth? Father Malone came to the infirmary to console us a little, and wishes to know if he can be of use.'

'Father Malone wasn't here when Sister Elizabeth died, was he?' Detective Sergeant Mill glanced at the prioress.

'I telephoned the presbytery and asked him to offer mass early,' she said.

'Then I doubt if he can add anything to what little information there is,' the detective said. 'As to the requiem – I'm afraid the body of Sister Elizabeth will have to be forensically examined before we can release her to the convent again, but I'll have the authorities make speed so as not to interfere with the funeral arrangements.'

'Oh, Sister Elizabeth won't mind,' Sister Hilaria said peacefully. 'She will be a little confused at the moment, of course.'

'Sister.' He bent forward slightly, his voice carefully neutral. 'Sister Elizabeth is dead, you know.'

'Very suddenly dead,' Sister Hilaria said. 'That is why she is now so confused. Our prayers will help her to settle happily on the other side.'

'Yes. Yes, of course.' He looked rather at a loss.

'I don't think that Sister Hilaria will have much to tell you,' Mother Dorothy said. 'She slept in my cell last night and as I didn't hear anything—'

'You didn't wake up during the night, Sister?' Detective Sergeant Mill asked.

'No, I slept soundly,' Sister Hilaria said.

'Thank you.' He sighed faintly as he made a note. 'Perhaps I could speak to Sister Perpetua now?'

'She went into the kitchen to prepare breakfast,' Sister Hilaria said.

'Sister Joan, if your presence isn't essential here perhaps you might take over the task?' The prioress glanced at her. 'I would like to stick as closely as possible to our normal routine. Detective Sergeant Mill, have your men finished in the lay cell?'

'Constable Petrie is overseeing things there. Sister Joan is free to go, of course.' Which meant, Sister Joan thought, genuflecting and withdrawing with Sister Hilaria in tow, that he didn't expect to learn anything at all from the rest of the community that might help to begin solving the case. Everybody had slept peacefully; nobody would have heard anything at all.

In the kitchen Sister Perpetua was slicing bread with swift, angry strokes, her gingery brows drawn down.

'They've just taken her away and locked the cell door,' she said in a tense, angry tone that hid the grief which Sister Joan was aware she'd never display. 'Poor little harmless soul! Well, no doubt they'll find out who did it. Since you're here, Sister, I suppose that means that Detective Sergeant Mill wants a word with me – not that it'll do any good. I slept like a log last night. Never heard a thing.' She took off her apron and went out.

Sister Joan went to the kitchen door and opened it. Outside the air was fresh and sweet. There was no sign of any ambulance but she guessed that it had pulled up nearer the main gates so as to avoid further upsetting the community. Poor Sister Elizabeth had left the convent as noiselessly as she had lived and died there.

She counted the slices of bread on to the large platter, checked that the kettle was simmering nicely and the two big coffee-pots ready, counted out pears into a bowl.

'Sister Joan, I'm going off now back to the presbytery.' Father Malone had come to the inner door. 'I shall tell Father Stephens what has happened here and then go on to the hospital. There will be prayers to be said there before anything else. This is a dreadful occurrence, Sister.'

'Yes, it is,' she said soberly, turning back into the kitchen. 'Have you had a cup of tea or coffee yet, Father?'

'Sister Perpetua was kind enough to give me one. I shall
come back later, Sister.' He drew a blessing upon the air and
went out.

Death or no death the routine had to continue as smoothly
as possible. Sister Joan closed the outer door and started
stacking coffee mugs on the big wooden tray. Sister Perpetua
came back in, some of the tension drained out of her.

'That young man knows his business,' she said briefly. 'I
must see to Sister Mary Concepta and Sister Gabrielle. Can
you manage the rest yourself?'

'Yes, of course, Sister. Who's in the parlour now?'

'Sister Martha who looks scared to death, poor child! As if
she could possibly be suspected of anything!'

'I don't think any of us are,' Sister Joan said. 'It must have
been someone from outside.'

'How did they get in?' Sister Perpetua demanded.

Sister Joan hesitated. The information that the door to the
chapel wing had been open when she first got up hadn't
evidently become common knowledge yet.

'It stands to reason,' she said at last. 'Nobody had any
reason to kill Sister Elizabeth.'

'From the community you mean? I suppose not.' Sister
Perpetua grunted an unwilling assent and went off again.

'But someone wanted her dead, Sister.'

Bernadette came in from the yard, carefully scuffing her
shoes on the mat.

'You went out?' Sister Joan looked at her.

'I couldn't stand just sitting indoors not knowing what was
going on,' Bernadette said earnestly. 'I went out to talk to the
pony.'

'So I see.' Sister Joan twitched a strand of straw from the
end of her braid.

'Animals are nicer than people sometimes, aren't they?'
Bernadette said.

'Sometimes I'm inclined to agree with you,' Sister Joan
admitted. 'Would you like to help me carry the food upstairs?
Everybody wll be coming up for breakfast soon. There's no

point in dwelling on what's happened unless we can do something about it.'

'I hate death,' Bernadette said, picking up the laden tray. 'I always hated death. People ought to live for ever if they feel like it!'

'I used to feel like that sometimes,' Sister Joan said.

Suddenly she felt — not elderly, but no longer quite so young. It was a sensation that was entirely new and unwelcome.

'Sister, may I have a word?'

This time it was Magdalen Cole, coming in and pushing the corridor door closed behind her. Her face was white, her eyes troubled.

'What is it?' Sister Joan started to pour boiling water into the jugs.

'It's my fault that Sister Elizabeth was killed,' Magdalen said in a whisper.

'What makes you say that?'

Astonished at her own presence of mind Sister Joan put down the heavy kettle with great care and turned to face the other.

'Because I opened the door into the chapel wing,' Magdalen said.

'Why didn't you tell Detective Sergeant Mill?' Sister Joan asked.

'I was scared.' Magdalen twisted her hands together. 'I woke up about — about two o'clock, I suppose. I'd had such a bad dream that I felt scared. Because of Sister Marie being attacked, I suppose. I've always been very sensitive. I was afraid to go back to sleep again straightaway so I slipped out of the put-u-up bed and put on my slippers and dressing-gown, and went into the hall. I thought it would be very calming to spend a little time in the chapel, so I unlocked the door and went through. It was peaceful there with just the sanctuary lamp burning. I sat down and said three Hail Marys, and then I went back to bed.'

'Without relocking the door?'

'I thought I had locked up again,' Magdalen said, 'but I was getting sleepy. I was getting very sleepy, and so it's possible that I forgot.'

'What about the others in the infirmary? Didn't they hear you get up?' Sister Joan asked.

'I don't think so, Sister. They were all fast asleep. Sister Gabrielle was snoring. And I was very quiet so as not to disturb them. If I hadn't left the door open then Sister Elizabeth would still be alive!'

'We don't know that for certain.' Sister Joan tried to speak kindly but she was shaken suddenly by temper at the other's stupidity. 'Anyway you'll have to tell the police, you know.'

'I couldn't!' Magdalen's voice had risen slightly. 'Not with Mother Dorothy there! If she knew I'd been so careless she'd send me away, Sister. I couldn't bear to be sent away from here! I truly couldn't bear it!'

Eight

Violent death had coloured the day despite all Mother Dorothy's efforts to maintain a semblance of normality. The police had gone, leaving the lay cell where Sister Elizabeth had died locked. Breakfast had been a silent, hurried meal. The bright day outside the grey walls mocked the uneasy silence within.

Sister Joan had dismissed Magdalen Cole with a few soothing words, more to conceal her own state of mind than to comfort the young woman. Inwardly she was seething at the stupidity that had left a door unlocked at a time when security measures were more important than usual. Neither was she sure that she altogether believed the tale. Magdalen had woken in fright but had been clear-headed enough to move noiselessly through the darkness so as not to disturb her sleeping companions, had sat in the deserted chapel knowing that the outer door was unlocked, and had said nothing to anybody about her nocturnal excursion.

For the moment she had decided not to say anything to Mother Dorothy but at the first opportunity she would certainly inform Detective Sergeant Mill. Withholding evidence was a serious offence. On the other hand if Magdalen was sincere in her desire to join the community then her own personal dislike of the intending postulant ought not to colour her actions.

Father Malone returned before lunch and was closeted with the prioress for over half an hour. Sister Joan, mucking out the stable, glimpsed him driving off and wondered what conclusions the priest had reached.

At lunch Mother Dorothy rose from her place after the soup and bread had been eaten, her voice clear and firm, her calm expression bringing a sense of security into the uneasy atmosphere.

'Sisters, what happened here is both sad and shocking, an intrusion of evil into the peace of the cloister. I know how difficult it must be for all of you to continue with our routine of work and prayer as if nothing had happened, how hard it is to maintain our customary silence when our minds teem with questions. Father Malone tells me that Sister Elizabeth will be brought back to us tomorrow morning, and then we can prepare her for burial in our customary manner. Notice of her death has been sent to our other houses, and there will be a requiem mass in the chapel the day after tomorrow. Two police photographers will be here this afternoon to take some extra photographs of the cell where she died and I understand that two constables are already searching the grounds for evidence of an intruder. Meanwhile we must try to go about our business in the usual way, confident that the murderer will be brought to justice and that Sister Elizabeth is now at peace. If any of you should recall some piece of information, no matter how trivial it might seem, please come and tell me about it at once so that I can pass it on to the police. Sister Joan, Father Malone wishes someone to drive down to the presbytery after lunch so that final arrangements can be made for the obsequies, and some additional flowers purchased to supplement our own offerings from the garden. Will it trouble you to go alone?'

'No, of course not, Reverend Mother,' Sister Joan said promptly.

'Surely someone ought to go with her?' Sister Mary Concepta ventured.

'It's kind of you to be concerned, Sister,' Sister Joan said, somewhat hastily, 'but I'm certain that I shall be in no danger at all. May I drive down in the van, Mother?'

Mother Dorothy sighed.

'It would certainly be better if the vehicle had been repainted,' she said, 'but since that task hasn't yet been embarked upon then there's no help for it. And it was most kind of Brother Cuthbert to offer it to us. You might stop by and see that Brother Cuthbert is all right on your way to the presbytery. Father Malone informed him of the recent tragedy but a further visit from yourself might be appreciated.'

'Yes, of course, Reverend Mother.' Sister Joan sat down again, aware that she hadn't asked leave to call in at the police station. To have requested permission to do so would have meant having to explain why, and until she had resolved the question with Detective Sergeant Mill she was reluctant to do anything that might get Magdalen into trouble.

Bernadette put up her hand, offering to wash the dishes, and with that chore lifted from her shoulders, Sister Joan excused herself and went down to the van. Its vivid surrealistic patterns clashed with the sombre mood of the day. Fastening her seatbelt conscientiously she lifted a hand to Sister Perpetua who was sweeping the yard and drove down to the main gates, passing two constables who, bent almost double, were carefully examining the grass verges.

Brother Cuthbert was outside the former schoolhouse, fiddling with the engine of the old convent car. As Sister Joan drew up he turned, revealing an oil-streaked face and wiping his hands on a rag before he came over to open the van door for her.

'This is a terrible affair, Sister.' His freckled young face was grave. 'Poor Sister Elizabeth! Father Malone was good enough to tell me what has happened and, of course, the police came.'

'Surely they don't suspect you!' Sister Joan exclaimed.

'Until the person responsible is caught they have to suspect everybody, I suppose,' he said. 'But they were more interested in asking me if I'd seen anyone going to the convent or, at any rate, in that direction, at any time during the night.'

'And did you?'

'I was fast asleep,' he said simply. 'I woke up at five as I always do and started my morning prayers out here. The air is so fresh and clear at that hour. If I didn't have prayers to say I'd probably be tempted to caper all over the place praising nature.'

'I hope you'll go on resisting the temptation,' Sister Joan said, amused, 'in case someone sees you and gets the wrong idea.'

'Oh, I do manage to restrain myself,' Brother Cuthbert said. 'The point is that I never saw anybody at all. I finished my prayers and decided to walk down to the parish church for mass for a change. Father Stephens offered it. He recites it most beautifully – the Liturgy, I mean. I walked back here afterwards and had some breakfast, and I didn't see anyone until Father Malone stopped off to tell me what had happened. Then a very pleasant police officer – Detective Sergeant Mill – came by to ask me some questions but I'm afraid I wasn't able to help him very much.'

'It's a dreadful business,' Sister Joan said soberly. 'If you do see anything that strikes you as unusual you'll mention it to the police?'

'Yes, of course, Sister, but the trouble is that I'm not a noticing kind of chap,' he said apologetically. 'A bit apt to woolgather. Father Prior never stops scolding me about it.'

An innocent who regarded the world as being as clean and clear as himself, Sister Joan thought, leaving him to delve into the old car again and climbing back behind the driving seat.

She would go to the presbytery first, she decided, and then to the police station. If the information she felt obliged to give wasn't considered of vital importance then, for the time being at least, she would say nothing to Mother Dorothy. It was clear that Magdalen was devoted to the idea of a religious life, and it would be unfair to cast any doubts on her character and possibly spoil her chances of entering the community.

Both priests were out, but Sister Jerome handed over a touching wreath of spring flowers that some of the local parishioners had already made, expressed regret in her dour way and retreated indoors without further comment. Sister Joan drove on to the police station, parked neatly and went in, still wondering if she was doing the right thing.

'Sister Joan, come in, won't you?'

Detective Seregant Mill had opened the door of his office.

'Thank you.' Entering, she was struck as always by the impersonal atmosphere of the room. Everything was neat, clean, almost bare. Today even the photograph of his two boys wasn't in its usual place.

'I gave Father Malone all the information I could supply concerning the return of Sister Elizabeth's body to the convent.' He gestured to a chair and sat down himself.

'Yes, I know. That isn't why I'm here.' She clasped her hands tightly together.

'And it isn't a social visit?'

'You know perfectly well that we don't run round paying social visits,' Sister Joan said, returning his smile. 'This has to do with – well, I've some information, Detective Sergeant Mill, and I feel you're the best person to have it.'

'And not your prioress?' He shot her a keen glance.

'I'm not sure.' Sister Joan hesitated. 'The problem is that I have information that might affect someone's life injudiciously if it became general knowledge.'

'I think,' he said easily, 'that you'd better tell me, don't you?'

'Our two guests – Bernadette Fawkes and Magdalen Cole – both of them wish to enter the novitiate. The final decision will be Mother Dorothy's, of course. The point is that these days postulants aren't expected to be Snow Whites but there are certain standards—'

'Why not give me the information and let me decide if it's relevant? I'm not concerned with personal morals, you know.'

'Magdalen has told me that she woke up during the night and went to the chapel to pray for a little while. She unlocked the inner door but she can't recall whether or not she relocked it on her way back to the infirmary. She assured me that she heard and saw nothing out of the ordinary but naturally she blames herself for having been so careless.'

'Did she tell you what time it was when she woke up?'

'At about two o'clock she said. Was Sister Elizabeth—?'

'She died between three and four thirty or thereabouts. We haven't found the weapon yet. She was struck ferociously across the forehead as she slept. She wouldn't have known anything about it.'

'So someone could have entered from the outside.' Sister Joan bit her lip.

'It seems probable.' Detective Sergeant Mill made a note on the pad before him and raised his head again. 'Miss Cole surely wouldn't be barred from entry because a careless act had had tragic consequences? What else have you to tell me?'

'Whoever grabbed Sister Marie might have thought he was grabbing Magdalen Cole since Sister Marie was wearing Magdalen's white headscarf. Sister Elizabeth slept in the lay cell where Magdalen's been sleeping.'

'The postulants wear pink gowns, don't they?'

'Yes, but perhaps Magdalen has a pink dress. I haven't asked her yet. It is possible that she was the intended victim, don't you think?'

'We've certainly considered it as a possibility,' he said. 'Have you any further reason for thinking so?'

'Magdalen Cole is afraid of somebody,' Sister Joan said.

'You recently came for a rape alarm. Was it for her?'

'Yes. Yes it was. She asked me not to say that it was for her.'

'Did she tell you exactly why she was frightened? Was she scared of any particular person, for instance.'

'She didn't say. Only that the convent was in a lonely place and she would feel safer if she could summon help quickly. I assured her that we were absolutely safe – a bit stupid of me in view of what's happened.'

'Nobody could have foreseen it,' he said.

'There is something else.' Sister Joan hesitated. She had

begun to tell Detective Sergeant Mill about the flick knife she had confiscated from Magdalen, but to own one was illegal. He might regard it as his duty to take official action.

'Yes?' He was looking at her.

'I don't like Magdalen Cole very much,' she said, hastily choosing a different topic. 'That's why I didn't say anything until now. I wasn't sure how prejudiced I was against her.'

'Whether you like her or dislike her doesn't alter the fact that you were quite right to tell me about her going into the chapel in the middle of the night. Your conscience is too tender, Sister.'

'My conscience,' she said ruefully, 'is the bane of my life sometimes. Well, I shall try to persuade Magdalen to tell Reverend Mother about her forgetfulness. I'm sure it won't make any difference to her entering the community. Thank you.'

'Don't go yet, Sister.' His gesture sent her back to her chair. 'Tell me about Sister Elizabeth.'

'Didn't Mother—?'

'Mother Dorothy gave me the official line – an orphan, no close relatives, a good, pure girl, an exemplary novice. I want the unofficial version. What was she really like?'

'There isn't an unofficial version,' Sister Joan said. 'She was exactly as Mother Dorothy described her. Very quiet and reserved, gentle in her ways. That sounds like an epitaph, doesn't it? Gentle in her ways. I don't think she ever broke a rule in her life.'

'She sounds dull,' Detective Sergeant Mill said.

'Yes. Yes, she was very dull,' honesty compelled her to admit.

He laughed suddenly, leaning back in his chair and raising a dark eyebrow. 'It never fails to astonish me,' he said, 'how you walk a tightrope between being the perfect nun and a woman with strong opinions of her own.'

'That's one of your less perceptive remarks,' she challenged. 'Surely you know by now that being a nun never stopped anyone from having strong opinions.'

'Then it must be the way you express them.' He sobered abruptly, leaning forward again. 'I asked you about Sister Elizabeth because it's useful to know as much as possible about the victim – unless it's a random attack, and even then the personality of the victim must play a part. But this wasn't a random attack by some deranged person. This murder was meant. And you tell me that nobody had any reason to harm Sister Elizabeth.'

'She might have been mistaken for Magdalen.'

'As Sister Marie was?'

'It was dark in her cell,' Sister Joan reminded him. 'Whoever opened the door could have gone in, delivered the blow that killed Sister Elizabeth, and left without knowing that he had the wrong person. Magdalen had volunteered to take the other lay cell when she first arrived, but when Mother Dorothy decided that we ought all to sleep in the main house because of the prowler, she offered to sleep on the put-u-up in the infirmary so that Sister Elizabeth could have the lay cell.'

'And everybody knew about that?'

'Yes, of course, but you don't really think one of the community killed Sister Elizabeth, do you?' she said, startled.

'Someone from outside might have mistaken Miss Cole for Sister Elizabeth in the dark, or the other way round – whatever! That presupposes that someone knew where Magdalen Cole was sleeping when she first arrived. Has she made any telephone calls? Written any letters?'

'Not as far as I know. If she is afraid of someone she'd hardly let them know where she was sleeping, would she?'

'Which brings us back to Sister Elizabeth who might have been the intended victim all along. You can see now why I asked you about her.'

'Nobody from the community would have killed her,' Sister Joan said firmly. 'Nobody from the community could possibly kill anybody. It's absurd!'

'Oh, we're all capable of murder sometimes.' He looked down at his hands.

'Of thinking about it. Not of carrying it out. I really ought to go now, Detective Sergeant Mill! I have to catch Father Malone at the presbytery. Some of the parishioners have been kind enough to donate a wreath and – oh, the roses!'

'Roses?'

'It probably hasn't anything to do with anything, but someone's been leaving roses all over the place – expensive hothouse roses.'

'Leaving them where exactly?'

'On the day that our guests arrived,' Sister Joan said hesitatingly as she cast her mind back, 'I thought that I heard an intruder up in the library over the chapel. I went up to check and someone rushed past me – swirled past me down the stairs and then was gone. I found a rose on the doorstep of the chapel the next morning. I'd taken the precaution of locking the outer door for once so I got up early to unlock it and the rose was there. There was another rose in the little washroom that leads off the library when I went to check later. They didn't come from our garden.'

'Did you report the prowler to Mother Dorothy?'

'No. No, I didn't. No harm had been done and I really didn't want to alarm her. Someone might have brought the roses as an offering for the altar and not wanted to be seen.'

'Come on now, Sister! You don't really believe that,' he said.

'I'm not certain what I believe,' she said, colouring slightly. 'I was confused because it was dark and – I know that I ought to have called one of the other sisters or turned on the lights or something, but I didn't. There was something – unreal about what was happening. What went past me was blackness against blackness, like a great bat.'

'Next time you ought to provide yourself with a bunch of garlic,' he mocked.

'It sounds ridiculous I know,' she admitted, 'but no harm was done. And by then Magdalen had made it pretty clear to me that she was nervous about someone or other. So I said nothing. Sorry.'

'Have there been any more roses?'

'Two. One was in the glove compartment of the van that Brother Cuthbert drove down from Scotland in. He bought it cheaply in Glasgow. The other one was in a jug on the table in the schoolhouse where he's staying. He thought that someone had put it there as a welcoming gesture.'

'Did he tell you who sold him the van?'

'He didn't say. He paid two hundred pounds for it.'

'We'll see if we can trace the owners. Roses.' Detective Sergeant Mill drew one thoughtfully on his pad. 'I can't see how they fit in, but you'll let me know if any more turn up?'

'Yes, of course. I should have said something before. Things seem to be happening so fast.'

'Too fast,' he said soberly.

'I'd better get back to the presbytery. I've taken up a lot of your time.'

'That went too quickly too,' he said. 'Sister, be very careful, won't you? Keep away from lonely places.'

'Yes, I will. Goodbye, Detective Sergeant Mill.' She shook hands more briskly than she felt and went out.

'Did you drive down here in the van?' He had followed her into the reception area.

'Yes.'

'Could you walk to the presbytery?' he enquired. 'I'd like the fingerprint boys to have a look at the vehicle.'

'Yes, of course. I'll walk there and walk back in about – half an hour?'

'That ought to be long enough – not that I'm expecting any results. Kids scrumping apples wear gloves these days,' he said.

Father Malone had returned and opened the door to her himself, clucking apology. 'I was called away – a baby to baptise in a hurry, but the little mite was already rallying when I finished the sacrament. That often happens, you know. The dying often revive and decide to go on living after they receive the sacrament of extreme unction. Come along in, Sister. Sister Jerome went over to the hospital to keep vigil beside Sister Elizabeth. They were very kind there, very discreet about all the sad forensic business. You'll have a cup of coffee?'

'Thank you, Father.'

Going into his comfortably cluttered study she remembered the bleakness of Detective Sergeant Mills's office.

'This is a terrible business, Sister.' He poured coffee and added cream and sugar with a generous hand. 'Now you drink that. Lent or no you need the extra energy!'

'Ought I to go to the hospital too, do you think?' she asked.

'Sister Jerome will manage very well. Not that a vigil will benefit poor Sister Elizabeth but I believe that mourning rites are more to comfort the living than anything else. Did you know the poor child had no close relatives?'

'Yes, I know.'

'Though I'm sure she looked upon you as her family,' he said kindly. 'And if she had neither kith nor kin then she wouldn't have found any difficulty in detaching herself from the personal friendships, so in that she was blessed.'

'But not in her death,' Sister Joan said.

'The doctor said that she could have known nothing about it. She went to sleep as usual and woke up in heaven. That can't be too bad, eh, Sister?'

'Not if you think so, Father,' Sister Joan said politely. Privately the idea horrified her.

'They'll bring her up to the convent by nine tomorrow morning. I've seen the coroner so that's all arranged. A biscuit, Sister?'

Sister Joan shook her head.

'Mother Dorothy sent down a novice's habit by me for Sister Elizabeth to be buried in,' Father Malone said. 'She felt that as the poor child was about to enter the novitiate it would be a nice gesture.'

'It must make Sister Elizabeth feel heaps better,' Sister Joan said, tersely. 'I'm sorry, Father. That was rude of me.'

'You remind me of my old mother back in Ireland,' he said,

unoffended. 'A tongue like nettles and a heart like roses. More coffee, Sister?'

'No, thank you, Father. About tomorrow—?'

'I'll come up as usual to offer mass and wait for Sister Elizabeth to be brought back. Brother Cuthbert would play for the requiem, I'm sure. That's a very nice young fellow.'

'Yes he is.' Thinking of Brother Cuthbert made her feel marginally more cheerful.

'Until tomorrow then, Sister. You didn't walk here?' Escorting her to the front door he looked out with some anxiety.

'I came in the van. It's parked – near the police station.'

'Drive carefully, Sister. Until this man is arrested it's as well to be cautious.'

'Yes, Father. I will.'

Walking up the street she resolved to drive very carefully. It was no business of hers that Detective Sergeant Mill had a bleak, impersonal office.

Constable Petrie met her in the station yard.

'Have you come for the van, Sister?' he asked. 'It's been dusted for fingerprints but there are so many prints, including, I'm sure, Brother Cuthbert's and your own that it'll take a week to eliminate them from the enquiry. Detective Sergeant Mill sends his regrets but he had some paperwork to finish.'

'Thank you, Constable Petrie.'

Was the detective also driving carefully? She climbed up into the van and closed the door.

'Don't forget your seatbelt, Sister!' The constable grinned and raised his hand in salute as she drove out into the street.

The rule of compassion for all but no special lay friendships was her emotional seatbelt, she reflected. Irritatingly restrictive at times but a protection against disaster.

Within sight of the schoolhouse she veered away, bumping over the grassy contours of the moor towards the rash of lorries and caravans that disfigured the horizon. The new-age

travellers were still here then, and apparently not causing any
bother, though she hoped they'd pick up their garbage before
they went.

She slowed down as a lanky frame topped by a ponytail
hailed her.

'Good afternoon, Wind.' She wound down the window
and smiled at him.

'Is it true one of your lot's been blown away?' he
demanded. 'We've had police round all day asking
questions.'

'One of the sisters had been killed, yes.'

'Hey, man! that's bad news.' His face had lengthened.

'Very bad,' she agreed sombrely. 'I take it that you weren't
able to tell the police anything useful?'

'Not a thing. We never met the sister. Are you getting out
to stretch your legs, Sister?'

'If I do,' she hesitated, 'will I come back to find the wheels
gone?'

'It'll be safe as my virginity, honest!' he said.

'In which case,' said Sister Joan, removing the ignition key
and climbing down, 'I shall be very wary of leaving it for
more than five minutes.'

'Are all the nuns here like you?' he demanded.

'They're much nicer than me.'

'The one who was killed?' He shot her a sideways glance.
'Have you any idea who did it?'

'An intruder. One of the other postulants was attacked in
the grounds but happily more shocked than hurt.'

'Didn't the guard dog bark?'

'Guard – oh, Alice! Alice is in kennels completing her
training at the moment. Anyway the enclosure is being very
closely watched at the moment.'

'You didn't have to say that you know,' he said. 'I'm not
the one who goes round attacking people.'

'And you've no idea who does?'

He shook his head, the ponytail swinging.

'And your friend – Julian?'

'He's not a real mate,' White Wind told her. 'We just teamed up together, that's all. Being out of work needs company.'

'And now you've both teamed up with Miss Dacre?'

'With Sylvia Dacre, yes.' He frowned suddenly, staring at the ground.

'She seems to be an interesting person,' Sister Joan said.

'She's cool. Keeps herself to herself. Doesn't interfere with us.'

'And when are you moving on?'

'Sounds like, "Lovely to see you! When are you going home?".'

'I wondered if you'd be allowed to leave the district, that's all.'

'Because of what's happened to the nun? We had to give names and addresses and get ourselves checked up on.'

'And where does White Wind live?'

'White Wind lives on his wits, baby.' He grinned at her. 'However Steve Conrad lives in ye olde family villa in Wimbledon. Don't ruin my reputation by spreading it all over the place, will you?'

'I won't say a word. What about your friend, Julian?'

'We met up at a gig last year and decided to meet up in Falmouth this year and hit the open road together. He was up north when the time came round so he hitched a lift with that brother who's arrived here.'

'Brother Cuthbert. Yes, he did mention it.'

'You're asking a lot of questions yourself, Sister.' His glance was sharp, suspicious. 'Are you undercover or something?'

'Just a nun with an overdeveloped bump of curiosity,' she said lightly.

'Was the nun a friend of yours?' he asked.

'She was one of my sisters,' she said.

'You fancy a beer, Sister?'

They had reached the caravan where she had first seen Sylvia Dacre seated on the steps. The last thing she fancied was a beer but she was curious about the occupants of that caravan and he was already pulling open the door and gesturing her within.

'Thanks. A beer would be nice.' She went up the steps into a surprisingly roomy interior dominated by a large mattress piled with vivid covers and cushions.

'Make yourself at home, Sister! I'll get a couple of cans.' He leapt back down the steps and threaded his way between the other vehicles.

She sat down on a stool which seemed to be the only other piece of furniture in the place, and looked round at the garments hanging in plastic bags against the walls, the wide sill with dishes stacked on it, the bunches of herbs that floated on hooks from the ceiling, the tarnished oil stove. The whole effect had a certain careless charm. Looking at the mattress she wondered how many shared it. Not that it was any of her business.

'Here we are! I've got you a straw too.' White Wind leapt up the steps again.

'Thank you.'

The beer was warm and left a tingling sourness on the tongue. She sucked a few drops up and slid it down by her side.

'Julian and I sleep under the caravan,' White Wind said.

'I didn't ask.' Sister Joan picked up the can and took another reluctant slurp.

'And there's nothing between us either. We're not gay.'

'I didn't ask that either.'

'Just for you to know, Sister. I like to play the field but Julian's getting over a broken engagement. The girl just dropped him flat and vanished. Hit him hard.'

'I'm sorry to hear it,' Sister Joan said, keeping the bland expression on her face as she put down the can again. 'Look, I really ought to go! They're expecting me at the convent and – no offence intended, but I really don't like leaving the van for long. I've an awful feeling that the lock isn't very secure.'

'I'll walk you back. Don't bother to finish the beer. It's pretty awful anyway.'

'Thank you.' She climbed nimbly down the steps again. 'Will you give my regards to your friends? I'm sorry to have missed them.'

'Oh, they're around here somewhere,' he said carelessly. 'Watch your step, Sister. Standards of hygiene aren't too hot here.'

'It shouldn't worry you if you're a free spirit,' she teased, sidestepping an odorous puddle. 'Thanks again for the beer. It was a nice thought.'

'You're welcome any time, Sister. Let me know if you need any grass.' He grinned, waved and loped off.

'Grass!' Sister Joan echoed his words aloud, gripped by apprehension. She'd put the marijuana that he'd pressed on her into the glove compartment. By now the police would have found it!

Clicking open the compartment she looked anxiously within. No grass there. Only a fresh red rose, dewy satin petals guarded by sharp curving thorns.

Nine

Celebrations were all different but funerals always seemed to be the same, no matter who was being buried. There was a pall of sadness that hung as heavily as fog over the community, a sense of guilt because one was still alive, an aching emptiness at the heart. Yet this funeral had an added ingredient: there was about it the sense of fear. Sister Joan, taking her turn to scatter earth on the grave, felt it strongly. It seemed to her that the other members of the community stood a little closer together, that eyes were lowered not out of respect but out of a shared apprehension. At a little distance outside the wall Detective Sergeant Mill and Constable Petrie stayed discreetly in the background. There were several of the local parishioners there and a sprinkling of Romanies with Padraic prominent among them. No sign on any of the new-age travellers. She had half expected White Wind to be there. It must have been him who had put the rose there – it might have been him, she corrected her thoughts. He had gone off to fetch the beer, which proved nothing but robbed him of an alibi.

'*In nomine patriset filius et*—' Father Malone's voice roused her.

She genuflected and crossed herself in unison with her sisters. Sister Elizabeth had been buried as quietly as she had lived, only her death had been violent and she had known nothing even of that.

Magdalen and Bernadette hadn't come to the funeral. They had been at the service but had stayed behind in the chapel

137

when the rest filed out. She wondered if it was delicacy or revulsion that had kept them away.

'This is a sad day for you, Sister.' Padraic had stepped forward to shake her hand fervently in token of his sympathy. 'Not that I ever caught more than a glimpse of Sister Elizabeth, but she was one of yours after all. My good wife would have come with me to pay her respects but she gets nervous in crowds. Has anyone any notion who did it?'

'We think probably an intruder.' Sister Joan glanced towards Mother Dorothy, received a nod of approval which conveyed leave to continue her conversation, and said, 'It was very kind of you to come.'

'Least we could do. If you want my opinion, Sister,' Padraic said, 'it'll be one of those travellers as like as not. Nasty types most of them and not a drop of good Romany blood among the lot of them. Unless Luther's right and it was something else.'

'Something else?' They had moved away from the burial enclosure and she looked at him sharply.

'You know Luther,' Padraic said deprecatingly. 'Harmless as a fly but apt to get peculiar ideas in his head! He likes taking a little walk at night from time to time and—'

'You mean he goes poaching,' Sister Joan said.

'A bit here, a bit there,' Padraic shrugged. 'He says there's a huge bat flies across the moor, just above the ground, swishing through the air.'

Unwilling she remembered the silent, dark library, the sense of something else holding its breath, the rush of air as the figure went past her and down the stairs.

'Sister Elizabeth was killed by a blow on the head,' she said severely. 'You ought not to encourage Luther's nonsense!'

'Aye, it's probably nonsense,' he agreed. 'Luther has more than a couple of screws missing though I'd only say it to you, Sister, seeing he's my cousin.'

'Have you mentioned it to the police?' she asked.

Padraic gave her a patient look. 'The police don't bother us and we don't bother them,' he said. 'We answered the particular questions they put but nobody asked about bats.'

'And Luther has a vivid imagination. Yes, I do see why you didn't say anything,' she said with resignation. 'Anyway Sister Elizabeth was killed by a human being.'

'Too good a name for anyone who'd harm a woman, nun or no,' Padraic said. 'It was likely a maniac.'

'Perhaps.' Sister Joan smiled as she turned back towards the main house, but the smile faded as Padraic walked off.

Not all killers were maniacs, she reflected. There were those who were simply evil and those who killed for a reason which had some basis in sanity. Someone had followed Magdalen Cole to the convent, someone whom she feared sufficiently to carry a flick knife against, to ask for a rape alarm. Whoever it was had left roses as – as a sign of devotion? Roses were for lovers not killers who crept through the dark to wield a savage blow. And this killer, maniac or not, had seized every chance to get into the convent.

'Good morning, Sister.'

Detective Sergeant Mill had caught up with her.

'Good morning.'

She answered primly, half expecting the comment when he said, 'Was the grass for you or Brother Cuthbert?'

'Someone thrust it on me,' she hastened to explain. 'I really didn't know what to do with it so I shoved it in the glove compartment.'

'Where we found it.'

'I'm sorry. I know I should have reported it,' she said contritely.

'We've more to worry us than a little heap of hash,' he said easily.

'You didn't find anything else in the glove compartment?'

'No. Should we have done?'

'There was a red rose there.'

'When did you find it?'

'After I'd been talking to White Wind – he's a lad who's travelling with his mate.'

'You certainly have a wide variety of acquaintances,' he

said, amused. 'When were you talking to him?'

'The day before yesterday, after I picked up the van from the station yard. I really am not sure why I drove over to where they're camped – curiosity, a hunch, I don't know. Anyway he invited me into the caravan and went off to get me a can of beer – warm beer,' she said, grimacing at the memory. 'When I got back in the van he asked me if I wanted any more – oh!"

'So it was White Wind who thrust the grass on you in the first place. Don't look so stricken, Sister. I'm not interested in that.'

'I suddenly remembered that I'd shoved the stuff into the glove compartment. So I opened it and there was the rose. If your men didn't find one then it must have been put there while I was in the caravan. The lock on the door isn't secure so almost anybody could have come along and put it there.'

'Including your friend, White Wind.'

'I suppose so,' she said reluctantly. 'He seems like a nice boy though, even if he does use a somewhat exotic name.'

'His name's Steve Conrad and his father's a highly respected doctor in Wimbledon,' Detective Sergeant Mill told her. 'The boy's sowing a few very mild wild oats before he settles down to something more productive. Was his mate there?'

She shook her head.

'But his mate – Julian something – he was recently jilted by his fiancée and took it rather hard.'

'It's astonishing how people will chat away to nuns and clam up when a member of the police force hoves into view! You think our murderer may have been a rejected lover? We'll check the two boys a little more carefully but this doesn't have the scent of a *crime passionel*. Where were your two guests this morning?'

'They stayed in the chapel. I haven't had the chance to talk to Magdalen Cole again yet.'

'I was thinking of having a word with her myself,' he said thoughtfully, 'but I'll wait a while.'

'Hoping she'll confide in me?' Sister Joan looked at him sharply. 'I won't be your stool pigeon, Detective Sergeant Mill! If she tells me anything in strict confidence I have to respect that.'

'What you have to do is help with enquiries if the opportunity arises,' he said with equal sharpness. 'It might help prevent a further murder.'

'Yes, of course. I'm sorry.'

'It looks as if we just had our first quarrel,' he said with a down-curving grin.

'I was being over-scrupulous, that's all,' she said. 'If Magdalen says anything to me that's pertinent to the case, of course I'll let you know. Now, if you'll excuse me – and thank you for coming. That was nice of you.'

'Common practice,' he said. 'Good day to you, Sister.'

Going through the front door she veered towards the chapel wing.

The two girls sat together, both with sombre dresses on and white headscarves. Bernadette rose as Sister Joan came in, tiptoed to her and said in a whisper, 'Magdalen hates funerals and she was scared to stay here by herself so I stayed with her. I hope nobody thought we were being disrespectful?'

'I'm sure they didn't,' Sister Joan said warmly. 'Go and get yourself a cup of coffee. Sister Perpetua will be in the kitchen.'

'This is a rotten business, isn't it, Sister?' Bernadette lingered to say.

'Yes, a really rotten business,' Sister Joan agreed.

Magdalen sat in her place still, head bent. Sister Joan genuflected to the altar and sat down beside her.

'Death is often frightening, isn't it?' she said in a low, conversational tone. 'Even to those who have faith it is scary to think of going on into something of which we know absolutely nothing.'

'Were there many people there?' Magdalen asked tensely.

'Not many. A few of the local people, some Romanies from the camp, a couple of policemen. Not many.'

'I didn't want to go,' Magdalen said. 'I went to my mother's funeral when I was little and I kept on crying and crying. I couldn't stop. If I see a funeral, even on television, then it brings it all back, you see.'

'Well, it's over now.' Sister Joan patted the girl's arm and changed the subject. 'It was kind of Bernadette to stay with you but there wasn't any reason for you to feel afraid here, you know.'

'No reason?' Magdalen turned wide grey eyes towards her. They were red rimmed as if she hadn't slept. 'No reason, Sister? How can you say that when someone got into the convent and through my carelessness? And today, with people coming and going, anyone might come!'

'Well, it's not likely,' Sister Joan said. 'Magdalen, have you said anything yet to Mother Dorothy about having forgotten to bolt the door when you woke up that night?'

'Have you?' Magdalen countered.

'No. I think you'd feel better if you did though. She must be wondering who did it.'

'And if she finds out then she might send me away.'

'I don't think she would. She's very fair minded. But it might relieve your own conscience.'

'You're right, Sister.' Magdalen heaved a sigh and straightened her shoulders. 'I'll tell her that I was careless and then I was too scared to say anything. Thank you.'

'And there isn't any use in being frightened all the time,' Sister Joan pressed. 'If you are scared of someone in particular then you ought to tell someone about it.'

She had pressed too hard. Magdalen made an impatient little movement and said, 'I'm not frightened of anyone in particular. Why should I be? I'm scared of – most women are scared these days with crazies running about!'

'A few, perhaps, but surely—?'

'It only takes one to make a murder,' Magdalen said, and rose abruptly. 'Thank you, Sister. I'll go and see Mother Dorothy the first chance I get.'

She sidestepped into the aisle, knelt briefly and hurried out. Sister Joan slid to her knees and began a troubled Hail

Mary. She was certain that Magdalen was lying, that there was someone who had followed her here, had mistaken first Sister Marie and then, more tragically, Sister Elizabeth for her, and might try again if he knew by now that his victim had been the wrong one.

At lunch-time Sister Elizabeth's death notice which had already been sent to the other houses of the Order was read out. A dry record of a brief and blameless life its very brevity added to its poignancy. Sister Elizabeth had done no harm, had had no known enemies and now was dead, suddenly, unlawfully.

'We will often remember with pleasure her time among us,' Mother Dorothy ended. Sister Joan doubted it. Sister Elizabeth had been too colourless, too lacking in personality to be remembered vividly for long.

'I do have one other announcement,' the prioress was continuing. 'On the night that Sister Elizabeth – died, one of us woke up and went into the chapel to pray, forgetting to bolt the inner door on her return. I have been approached concerning this matter and can tell you that it's been cleared up to my satisfaction, so the subject is closed.'

It was impossible to see Magdalen's expression clearly from the end of the table. Sister Joan kept her own gaze lowered to her plate as did the others. Her own downcast lids hid anger. If the stupid girl hadn't been so careless then Sister Elizabeth might still be alive. She reminded herself that Magdalen was feeling worse about it than anybody else and ought to be pitied but the anger remained.

It was not customary to go on mourning for a long time. One couldn't hold back the dead with selfish tears when they had completed their journey. Two masses, the number of years she had spent in the Order, would be offered for her soul and after that she would be included among the souls of the faithful departed in the general prayers, her grave carefully tended by Sister Martha, her spiritual diary read by the prioress in case it contained words of wisdom to be passed on to those remaining. Sister Joan guessed that it wouldn't contain anything at all.

'Sister, would you like me to make a vegetable casserole for supper?' Sister Perpetua enquired, coming into the kitchen after lunch.

'Oh, would you, Sister? That would be marvellous!' Sister Joan said eagerly. 'I've been racking my brains, thinking what on earth to give everybody.'

'I'll make my special cheese sauce,' Sister Perpetua said. 'We need something to cheer ourselves up a bit. Can you bring me some carrots and turnips from the garden? Sister Martha's there with Bernadette, I think, so it'll be quite safe.'

'Yes, Sister.'

Going out, a basket on her arm, Sister Joan hoped that they'd get back to normal before long. It irked her spirit to be constrained by fear in the very place where they ought to feel most secure.

There was no sign of either Sister Martha or the pigtailed Bernadette. She hesitated, then went on through the gate into the garden. Beyond the further wall Sister Elizabeth's grave was a bare mound of earth with the wreath from the parishioners and some spring flowers from the convent grounds laid on top. By the time spring was warmed into summer the bare soil would be quick with grass.

A flicker of movement caught her eye. Someone had moved across her line of vision beyond the garden near the shrubbery that hid the old tennis court from view. It was probably one of the policemen, she decided, and wondered if it had been Detective Sergeant Mill who had ordered the surveillance.

The movement came again and on impulse she set off across the garden, rapidly threading her way between the vegetable beds and hurrying down the path that snaked across the rough grass between the angled shrubbery. The movement had ceased but she stood now at the top of the steps leading down to the tennis court. At the far side the severe lines of the postulancy rose behind its guarding wall. The windows were shuttered, the gate latched.

A sudden sound from the shrubbery startled her like a pistol shot. Without pausing to investigate she leapt down the steps two at a time and, empty basket wildly swinging, found herself running panic stricken across the moss-grown court, past the broken, sagging nets, through the gap in the wall and, without remembering having unlatched the gate, stood before the blank, unyielding façade of the old building.

Her heart was pounding. She turned to look back across the tennis court to the steps at the far side, and saw nothing moving at all. Only a faint breeze stirred the branches of a holly bush to which scarlet berries still clung in defiance of the death of winter.

'Joan, you're an idiot!' She spoke aloud, hearing her voice echo queerly in the little yard.

But she had seen something! A movement ahead, a sound behind as she hurried forward, a sense even now that someone watched her. She took a tighter grip on the basket and turned to face the house again. It was only a few days since Sister Hilaria and her two postulants had moved with Sister Teresa to the main house but this building already had the air of a dwelling long since deserted. It was all imagination of course but if buildings had feelings then this one was lonely.

Now that she was here she might as well have a look round, satisfy herself that nobody had trespassed, tried to break in. She stepped with conscious briskness around the corner, aware that she was humming a tune under her breath like a child whistling against the dark, and walked into a taller bulky figure.

The breath left her body in a swoosh of terror and she stood gasping.

'I'm so sorry, Sister, but I rather think that I'm on private ground.' Sylvia Dacre stepped back, looking down with a mixture of surprise and apology on her fine-boned features.

'Yes. Yes, you are.' Sister Joan found her voice though it emerged in a strangled squeak.

'I took a long walk and decided to deviate from the track. Where exactly am I?' Sylvia Dacre asked.

'On convent land. This is the postulancy.'

'Where the trainees live?' The other turned to look up at the shuttered windows.

'The trainees, yes. They stay here for about two years before they join the rest of us in the main house.'

'And then?' The other woman looked curious.

'They spend a year as a novice proper, helping out in the kitchen and carrying on with their studies and then they have a year's retreat before they take their final vows.'

'Which you have done, Sister – Joan, isn't it?'

'I'm Sister Joan, yes.'

'The boy – the one who calls himself White Wind has spoken of you.'

'He's a nice person,' Sister Joan said.

'He and his friend,' Sylvia Dacre said. 'Amusing young people.'

'You invited them to travel with you?'

'Nice to have company.'

Sylvia Dacre had a curious way of answering questions by some oblique, vaguely linking comment.

'You weren't old friends then?' Sister Joan pursued.

Sylvia Dacre shook her head. Greying strands of black hair fell from beneath the brim of a felt hat that was pulled almost down to her eyebrows. Forty-five? Less? It was difficult to guess her age. Her accent was cultured but her hands were earth-stained, callouses clear on the pads of the long fingers.

'When I decided to travel,' she enlarged, 'I felt that it might be safer to find a congenial travelling companion. It would discourage unwanted advances from less desirable people who have elected to share the same lifestyle.'

She didn't look as if she would be in need of any help in repelling any unwanted advances, Sister Joan thought, a gleam of amusement lightening the last of her terror. Sylvia Dacre was tall and, though slimmer than her bulky clothes and cape revealed, obviously strong and wiry.

'Yes. I suppose so,' she said aloud.

'But the travelling life wouldn't appeal to you?' Sylvia

Dacre smiled. She had rather a charming smile.

'People in the religious life are generally based in one place for long periods,' Sister Joan said.

'In a consecrated space which I have now violated.' The smile flashed out again. 'I apologize, Sister Joan. Is there any short cut I can take to avoid trespassing further? I took the long way round, I'm afraid, and I don't fancy such a hike back.'

'Would you like to come into the kitchen and sit down for a few minutes?' Sister Joan asked, somewhat belatedly recalling the rules of hospitality. 'We can give you a cup of tea.'

'That's very kind of you but I think not. I wouldn't be at ease in a convent,' the other said. 'And haven't you had a death here? I'd not wish to intrude.'

'Sister Elizabeth was buried this morning.'

'The sister was killed. The police took our names and addresses and asked if anyone had any information. Nobody had.'

'It was a dreadful event.'

'Yes indeed.' Sylvia Dacre hesitated, then said, 'The sister was a postulant, I understand. The detective sergeant mentioned it. I suppose it would discourage new entrants to the Order if the unfortunate girls were in danger of being murdered.'

'They certainly are not!' Sister Joan said with some spirit. 'Such events are almost unknown, thank God! Not that we get flocks of postulants either – religious vocations are dwindling these days.'

'But you still have girls coming to test the spiritual waters?'

'Yes, of course.'

They had begun to walk slowly across the tennis court. Overhead a returning emigrant bird shrilled loudly.

'Yes. There are always some vocations,' Sister Joan said.

'Have you any intending postulants with you now?'

The question was asked too artlessly, too casually. It made the hairs at the back of her head quiver slightly.

'We never discuss the internal affairs of the Order,' she said.

'One reason why I would feel awkward inside a convent,' Sylvia Dacre said. 'So much secrecy! You mentioned a short cut, Sister?'

She hadn't but with some relief she indicated the shrubbery at the top of the shallow steps.

'If you go behind there you come out onto the moor again not very far from where the new-age travellers are camped. It's a twenty-minute walk,' she said.

'Then I'll say goodbye, Sister.'

Her hand was suddenly enveloped in a bone-crushing grip. Dark eyes stared down at her with something avid in their depths. Then Sylvia Dacre loosened her grip and strode ahead, not turning her head, the black cape hanging heavy to her ankles in the windless air.

Sister Joan drew a long breath and let it out slowly. For no reason she could immediately fathom her forehead was damp with perspiration.

There were still the vegetables to gather. She went up the steps, resisted the temptation to explore the shrubbery and was pulling carrots when Sister Martha came up to her.

'I saw you from the window, Sister,' she said breathlessly. 'I thought I'd better run out and join you since you were alone.'

'And quite safe I assure you,' Sister Joan said. 'You were in the garden earlier.'

'No, Bernadette was supposed to come and help me, but I couldn't find her anywhere. You haven't seen her, I suppose?'

'No. No, I haven't. Not since lunchtime. Perhaps she's in chapel or in her room?'

'I looked in both places,' Sister Martha said.

They looked at each other silently.

'Help me get some vegetables for the supper,' Sister Joan said at last, 'and then we'll both search for her. I'm sure she's around somewhere. After all it's broad daylight!'

'Yes, of course.'

Sister Martha bent and tugged at carrots with her small, square hands, her spectacles slipping down her nose.

'Carrots, potatoes, swedes and turnips.' Sister Joan straightened up. 'Let's put them in the kitchen and go look for Bernadette.'

'Perhaps she went for a walk,' Sister Martha said as they panted round to the back door. 'She doesn't have to ask permission.'

'But surely she'd have told somebody!'

They had reached the yard, lugging the basket between them. From the open door of Lilith's stable came a loud whinny.

'What's wrong, girl?' Sister Joan surrendered her part of the burden and went across to look inside.

To her intense relief Bernadette was there, stroking Lilith's velvety nose, turning her head slightly in the dim straw-coloured light.

'It's all right, Sister Martha. Bernadette's here!' She raised her voice slightly, acknowledged Sister Martha's answering wave and turned back into the stable.

'I was supposed to go and help out in the garden,' Bernadette said.

'It isn't important. There's never very much to do once the spring planting and sowing are over. Are you all right?'

She asked the question sharply as a sudden shaft of light revealed a woebegone face with the unmistakable traces of tears on the cheeks.

'Yes. No. I'm not sure,' Bernadette said in rapid succession.

'Pick the right answer and you get a prize?' Sister Joan said, gently teasing. 'If anything's worrying you then it's sometimes true that two heads are better than one.'

'I don't know what to do, Sister Joan, and that's a fact.' Bernadette moved away from the stall and sat down disconsolately on a bale of hay.

'About what?'

'About applying to enter the Order,' Bernadette said.

'Oh, everybody feels like that,' Sister Joan said in relief.

'Merely coming in as a postulant doesn't commit you for life, you know. You can leave at any time during the first two years.'

'I just don't feel that I can live up to the standard, not when I'm so full of hate!' Bernadette burst out.

'Hate's a strong word.' Sister Joan sat down on the three-legged stool at a little distance. 'You don't strike me as a hating kind of person.'

'I hate Magdalen Cole,' Bernadette said low and fierce. 'I know it's wrong, Sister. Even if I wasn't thinking of becoming a nun it's still wrong! I never hated anybody I knew before – I mean we can hate Hitler and Genghis Khan and – well, hate what they did anyway, but it's easy to feel like that about someone you've only read about in books. I've met Magdalen and I wasn't keen on her from the start and now I loathe her and if she's coming here then I couldn't stand it!'

'For heaven's sake, what's happened?' Sister Joan demanded.

'After lunch Mother Dorothy asked if I'd step into her parlour for a moment,' Bernadette said. 'I went in and she said that I wasn't to worry about not being accepted here as a postulant, that she understood I'd been scared to mention that I'd gone downstairs on the night that Sister Elizabeth was – well, she said that anyone could forget to lock a door and I was to forgive myself, but that in future when I did anything wrong it was much wiser to go to her myself and not ask Magdalen or anyone to do it for me. Well, I can certainly forgive myself, Sister, because I slept all night through and never stirred but I'm damned if I can forgive Magdalen Cole for landing me in the stew like that. She's one of the sneakiest people I ever met!'

'What did Mother Dorothy say about it?'

'I didn't say anything about it,' Bernadette said. 'I couldn't.'

'Couldn't snitch on Magdalen Cole?'

'Not on anybody,' Bernadette said. 'Anyway I was just too shocked to say anything. I just sat there like a fool while

Mother Dorothy went on about not fretting over being careless. I couldn't say a word.'

'It was Magdalen who woke up and went into the chapel, of course, and then forgot to relock the door when she came back.'

'I figured that out already,' Bernadette said resentfully. 'She's so scared that she won't be accepted for the postulancy that she doesn't mind who she lands in the shit – sorry but that's how I feel, Sister!'

'At least it hasn't affected your own chances,' Sister Joan said cheeringly.

'It wouldn't have affected Magdalen's either if she'd owned up,' Bernadette said. 'Anyway it's shown me that I'm not the sort of person who can turn the other cheek. That doesn't make me the ideal candidate for the religious life, does it?'

'I've often thought that maxim was unfinished,' Sister Joan said. 'I mean if you turn the other cheek and get hit again there's nothing telling you not to stick up for yourself. If I were you I'd stop being so hard on myself. Mother Dorothy is a shrewd judge of character, you know. Sooner or later she'll realize what Magdalen Cole is all about. I know it's hard advice but I'd forget it if I were you. After all Reverend Mother didn't name you.'

'I bet she wishes she had,' Bernadette said darkly, and grinned suddenly. 'All right, Sister. I'll try not to let it bother me. Maybe Magdalen was just so scared of not being accepted that she heaped the blame on me without thinking of the consequences. Thanks for listening to me anyway.'

'Any time!' Sister Joan said, rising and extending her hand to Bernadette. 'Go and wash your face and then see if Sister Perpetua needs any help. She's making one of her special dishes for supper and if she sees me in the kitchen she'll be – what is it?'

'There's something under the straw here.' Bernadette who had also risen stooped to tug it out. 'It stuck into my leg as I moved.'

'It's a trowel. Sister Martha mentioned she was missing

one.'

Sister Joan took the tool, glanced down and froze. The short iron handle she was holding was clogged with blood to which a few hairs adhered, dark stained in the dim dust-laden light.

Ten

'Bernadette, don't say anything about this.' Sister Joan spoke tensely, resisting the temptation to drop the trowel. 'I'm going to take it down to the police station myself. If the police arrive here again and start questioning everybody then – well, I just feel it'd be better to keep quiet about this for the moment.'

'I won't say a word.' Bernadette was staring at it with dilated eyes. 'Is that the—?'

'There's dried blood on it still and a few hairs.'

'I thought the postulants had to shave their heads,' Bernadette said.

'When they first enter, yes, but after they've completed a year in the postulancy they start growing their hair a little again. Sister Elizabeth's had grown quite fast.'

Fine lank brown hair, she remembered, wisps of it poking from under the short veil in which she'd been buried.

'Do you want company?' Bernadette enquired.

'No, you stay and help Sister Perpetua. I don't want to make a big issue out of this.'

She had already handled the trowel so it probably made little difference to it if she covered it with her capacious sleeve, chivvying the younger woman towards the kitchen while she herself went to the parlour where, to her relief, she found Mother Dorothy poring over the parish magazine.

'Into town again! Is it absolutely necessary, Sister?' Her superior greeted her request with raised eyebrows.

'I think so, Mother.' Sister Joan drew the trowel from her

sleeve and laid it on the desk.

'Where did you find that?' Mother Dorothy asked sharply.

'Hidden in the stable, Mother. I thought it might be more discreet if I took it down to the station myself.'

'Yes. Yes, we don't want to alarm the community by a continued police presence,' Mother Dorothy said slowly. 'Was anyone with you when you found it?'

'Bernadette was in the stable too.'

'And she'll say nothing. That's a very nice girl,' Mother Dorothy smiled slightly. 'She has character. That's important in a religious.'

'Yes she has,' Sister Joan said, as significantly as she dared.

'Not, I believe, the type to persuade someone else to make her confessions for her.' Mother Dorothy smiled again, pushed her spectacles higher on her small nose, and said, 'You will not of course chatter about this, Sister.'

'Of course not, Reverend Mother. Thank you.'

'You had better put that in a plastic bag before you replace it up your sleeve. I have a bag here. Now that you've handled it you had better volunteer your fingerprints to the police. Come back as soon as you can.'

She spoke in a dry, emotionless manner. Only the faint puckering of her mouth betrayed distaste and regrets.

Sister Joan went out and got into the van, slipping the plastic-sheathed trowel under her seat before she started the engine. To her relief no questioning Sister Perpetua came to the door of the kitchen and she gained the open track without seeing anybody.

Mother Dorothy had drawn the correct conclusions regarding Magdalen's little burst of confidential information. One day she'd tell Bernadette about it no doubt but choose her own time and method. Sister Joan gave a little nod of satisfaction and drove faster, bumping over the turf past the old schoolhouse where there was no sign of Brother Cuthbert.

She was parking the van and slipping the trowel back into her sleeve when Constable Petrie came over to open the door for her.

'Good afternoon, Sister. If you're wanting the Detective Sergeant I'll run and head him off for you,' he said. 'He was just going off for an hour.'

'If you would, please. It's important.'

Heading for the office she felt a twinge of amusement, wondering if any other nun visited the local police station so often.

'Sister.' Detective Sergeant Mill favoured her with a curt nod as he ushered her in. 'Petrie says it's important.'

'New evidence,' Sister Joan said equally briefly and laid the trowel on the desk.

His expression changed as he looked at it.

'Sit down, Sister. Excuse my abruptness. I was in a foul mood because we seem to be getting precisely nowhere with this investigation,' he said. 'Where did you get this?'

'I found it in the stable hidden under the straw. Mother Dorothy agreed that it was wiser to bring it here rather than have the place crawling with police again.'

'Very tactfully put, Sister!' He laughed, visibly relaxing as he sat down at the desk.

'Sorry! I didn't mean it quite like that.'

'I bet you did. I'm afraid that we'll have to do more crawling very soon in view of this. When did you find it?'

'Less than an hour ago. I came straight here as soon as I had permission.'

'The stable was searched for the murder weapon,' he said. 'Either one of the lads fell down on the job which is highly unlikely or our killer's been back to hide the weapon in the stable after the search was called off. We thought it likely that the murderer had taken the weapon away with him.'

'It's a trowel belonging to the convent. Sister Martha mentioned having missed it a couple of days ago. I'm afraid that nobody took much notice at the time.'

'I suppose your prints are all over it by now?'

'Mine and Bernadette Fawkes's prints. She was sitting on the hay when she found it.'

'So everybody knows by now that it was found?'

'No. Bernadette won't say anything about it and I took it straight to Reverend Mother. She gave me the plastic bag.'

'Then we'll want your prints, Sister, and Bernadette's too in the near future. I've a feeling those are the only prints we'll find on it,' he said.

'But why hide it in the stable?' she asked. 'Whoever – used it could have cleaned it and put it back into the garden shed with all the other tools. The shed's not locked. Why hide it where it's bound to be discovered?'

'I don't know yet. Maybe someone wanted to direct attention towards the convent.'

'To make people think that one of us killed Sister Elizabeth? But why would anyone do that? It's crazy!'

'Not if the object was to deflect attention away from the intended victim,' he said.

'Yes, I see. Nobody in the convent had met Magdalen until recently so there wouldn't have been any reason for killing her, but there might have been a reason for killing Sister Elizabeth. Not that there ever was! Detective Sergeant Mill, do you think that Magdalen Cole is still in danger?'

'It's certainly likely,' he said. 'I've talked over the phone to her parish priest who doesn't seem to know her very well; he vaguely recalls her asking him for a reference. She rents a bedsitting room in London, has been there about six months, drawing dole money and getting her rent paid by Social Security. Described as quiet, shy, no close friends. Nothing known yet of her family. In the past she's done some secretarial work up north so we're checking on that. We haven't come across a lover yet.'

'So you'll be coming round to question us all more fully.'

'Now the funeral is over then we'll be stepping up investigations,' he confirmed. 'I'll get this to the path. boys and you can leave us your fingerprints. We'll get Miss Fawkes's dabs later.'

'And you think the killer wore gloves?'

'Almost bound to have done. There isn't much blood as you can see. Sister Elizabeth died of multiple fractures of the frontal lobes. The bones were driven inward so there wouldn't have been much blood. Have you had any visitors to the convent in the last couple of days?'

'I've seen Sylvia Dacre,' Sister Joan remembered. 'Early this afternoon I went out to pick some vegetables. She was by the postulancy, said she'd been walking and strayed on to convent ground. We chatted for a few minutes and I showed her a short cut.'

'She didn't go near the stable?'

Sister Joan shook her head. 'She was coming from the opposite direction,' she said. 'There's one other thing, Detective Sergeant Mill, I told you that something went past me down the library stairs and that it reminded me of a huge bat? Luther from the Romany camp told his cousin, Padraic, that he'd seen a big black bat rushing across the moor above the ground. No, I know that couldn't be so, but it does sound rather like my own experience, don't you think?'

'I'll bear it in mind. Come and have your prints taken. Then I'll make up for my earlier bad mood and buy you a coffee. I don't suppose you've had lunch?'

'I've had lunch and, if I'm not too late, I'll eat supper too.'

'Coffee then.' He rose, taking the plastic-wrapped trowel carefully between finger and thumb.

Having her prints taken made her feel faintly guilty of crimes she would never have dreamed of committing. Detective Sergeant Mill had told her once that most law-abiding people felt exactly the same way.

'Wipe your fingers, Sister.' He came in, nodding briskly to the constable in charge. 'If you don't mind canteen coffee we'll have it now and then I'll see you home.'

'There's no need,' she protested, allowing him to lead her up the stairs to the plastic and chrome area where drinks and snacks were served. 'I drove over in the van and I can drive back perfectly safely. It's scarcely twilight yet!'

'And there's someone out there who's already killed once. You ought to take better care of yourself, Sister Joan.'

'I do,' she argued as he placed the brimming mug before

her. 'It's just that I won't let my whole life be ruled by fear. That wasn't why I entered the religious life.'

'It was because you broke off your engagement, wasn't it? You mentioned it sometime.'

'Not an engagement. Jacob was Jewish and I wouldn't – couldn't convert.'

'A bit drastic rushing into a convent, wasn't it?'

'Jacob wasn't the only reason. I hadn't been in the postulancy for five minutes before I realized that I was in exactly the right place for me.'

'And Jacob?'

'Oh, he's probably married by now with two or three children,' she said lightly.

'How did you meet?'

'At art college. You must stop encouraging me to chatter about my life before I entered the order, Detective Sergeant Mill! It isn't encouraged.'

'Never look back,' he said thoughtfully, stirring his coffee.

'Something like that, but in your case—'

'We weren't talking about me.'

'Fair's fair,' she said, still lightly. 'Sometimes, when a relationship's going wrong, then it does make sense to look back and remember the good times.'

'You're a romantic, Sister.'

'Oh, I do hope so!' she exclaimed, and coloured up as he laughed.

'I'll see you to the van,' he said. 'I'll send Petrie up to take Bernadette Fawkes's prints very discreetly. If there are any others on the trowel that don't match yours or hers then we'll have to throw the net wider.'

'Have you got anyone watching the convent?' she asked as they went down the stairs into the yard again.'

'Not since last night. Mother Dorothy is of the opinion that the killer has left the district already. The trouble is that we're pretty short-handed anyway, and I can't spare enough men to patrol the grounds and keep an eye on the buildings as well. Has Mother Dorothy kept up the security precautions?'

'For the moment,' she told him, 'but sooner or later Sister Hilaria and Sister Marie will have to return to the postulancy. Sister Teresa too. It's not long to her final profession.'

'For the moment will have to do then, Sister. The light's fading fast. Are you sure you don't want an escort?'

'Positive. I'll be fine.'

'Drive carefully then. 'Bye, Sister.'

He raised his hand and turned away. Going back to collect whatever he needed from his bleak office, she supposed.

Street lights were flickering on, curtains being drawn, husbands hurrying home. She turned into the main street, slowing as Father Malone came round the corner and waved to her.

'Sister Joan, nothing wrong, I hope?' His worried face appeared at the window. She braked hastily and opened the window wider.

'Nothing's wrong, Father. I had an errand at the police station, that's all.'

'Could you perform a small favour for me on your way back?' he asked. 'I'd not want to be making you late for your supper, Sister, but—'

'Yes, of course, Father. What is it?'

'Sister Jerome made some pies and I promised to see that Brother Cuthbert got a couple. If you're going past—'

'I'll drop them off for you, Father. I'll put them on the seat.'

'I'll nip home and get them.' The worried expression had been replaced by a beam as he trotted off.

Sister Joan turned into the road where church and presbytery were situated. Ahead of her she could see Father Malone hurrying towards the front door. Beyond him there was a flicker of movement distorted by the shadows cast by the street lamp at the gate. Someone moved away and walked rapidly to the corner. Sister Joan glimpsed the distinctive black cape and white face as Sylvia Dacre turned her head and then was gone again into the shadows beyond the light.

'Here we are then!' Father Malone was coming back to the

side of the van. 'The pies are nice and juicy Sister Jerome said and he's to bring back the dishes when he's finished them both up. Drive carefully. There's quite a nasty mist rising.'

'I will, Father.'

Closing the window again, checking that the door was firmly shut and as securely locked as the current state of the vehicle permitted, she reversed and drove back to the main road.

It had definitely been Sylvia Dacre there, standing just past the gate, turning to hurry away as Father Malone approached. The woman seemed to turn up at regular intervals like the chorus of a Greek play, to silently point the action.

Turning off the road onto the moorland track she had driven only a few yards when she was engulfed in whiteness. It blotted out the rapidly darkening evening. It blotted out everything. She slammed on the brakes and sat for a moment, peering ahead. For two pins she'd turn back towards the friendly lights of the town but that would have been foolish when she knew the track so well, and when she usually wasn't nervous at all.

She drew a deep breath, deliberately released her tight grip on the wheel and drove slowly and cautiously, her headlights parting the white mist for no more than a few feet ahead.

A momentary break in the whiteness showed her the schoolhouse, appearing like something out of a fairy-tale before the whiteness closed in again.

'Brother Cuthbert! Brother Cuthbert?'

Leaving the lights struggling against the mist she climbed down, grasped the two neatly wrapped pies and went up to the closed door.

'Brother Cuthbert!' She raised her fist and knocked loudly.

Odd how mist distorted not only the seen but the heard. Her voice echoed queerly into a damp and dripping silence.

Her hand fell to the handle and she opened the door, her eyes slowly accustoming themselves to the more familiar darkness within.

'Brother Cuthbert?'

Within doors her voice echoed even more hollowly. Anyway it was stupid to go on calling when it was obvious Brother Cuthbert wasn't there. There was a lamp on the windowsill in what had been the classroom and was now the living-room-cum-bedchamber. She felt her way to it, barking her shin painfully on a chair, her hands reaching for the familiar curving bowl of the lamp and the box of matches that was next to it. An instant later she had a steady flame burning and the darkness was mellowed by warm golden light.

The bed had been neatly made and the fireplace was swept clean, bare of fuel or twigs. He had obviously gone out and delayed his return because of the mist. Normally she would have felt exasperation at his failure to lock the front door but now she was glad of it. She put the two pies on the table and looked round for something on which to leave a note but there was no paper or pen in sight and she disliked the notion of rummaging among his few possessions. In any case Father Malone would ask him if he'd enjoyed the pies when they next met. Now if she only knew whether or not Brother Cuthbert had a torch she could borrow it – but if he did have one then he'd probably taken it with him. The thought of borrowing the lamp instead occurred to her and was instantly dismissed. He'd need that when he got home.

What she could do was stay safely here until he did return but by then supper would be long over and the rest of the community would be worried. She turned down the wick of the lamp until it was no more than a glimmer, set it on the windowsill again, and went out, closing the door behind her and making her way to the blurred circles of light that denoted the van was still there.

Climbing up into the driving seat again, fastening her seatbelt, she rubbed the inside of the windscreen with a cloth but managed only to smear the glass.

'Oh – hang!' She wished that it was permitted to say something more colourful, more suited to her exasperation.

Perhaps a prayer to St Christopher would help. She sent up a brief prayer and started the engine. Provided she crawled along the track she would reach the main gates and drive of the convent without any trouble.

The engine spluttered into life and died. Biting her lip she tried again and had the same result.

The van had plenty of petrol. She tried to recall when she had last filled up the oil and couldn't remember.

'Thank you very much, Saint Christopher!'

Feeling extremely irritable, which was better than being scared, she climbed down again from the seat, closed the door, and set off on foot. She had no more than a couple of miles to walk.

The mist was, if anything, thicker. It clung to her habit and veil, made her want to cough in order to clear her lungs. After a few yards she stopped, telling herself that it was ridiculous to go on without any light to guide her or warn others of her presence. Turning, she groped her way back to the schoolhouse, opened the front door and, with a feeling of immense relief, secured the lamp, turning up the wick.

Brother Cuthbert would have to manage with a candle if he returned this evening. She sent up another short petition to St Christopher, added one to St Michael for good measure, and went out into the mist. She had switched off the van's headlights and the van itself was almost indistinguishable from the surrounding whiteness. She skirted it carefully, checked that her feet were on the rough track and began to walk on steadily within the little circle of radiance provided by the lamp.

The mist muffled the little sounds of the moor as the landscape settled down for the night. There wasn't even the rustle of a mouse in the grass to accompany the steady tread-tread of her sensible low-heeled shoes.

There was a change in the quality of the silence. She stood still for a moment, trying to analyse what it was that made her heart beat faster. It was as if, all around her, the whiteness listened too.

Something whooshed past her, so close that she felt the rush of air. Stumbling back, raising the lamp, she caught a glimpse of the huge bat-like creature that seemed to glide at a little distance above the ground and then the figure was gone, swallowed up.

With an almost objective interest she noticed that the lamp was shaking violently in her hand, sending beams of light darting wildly here and there. She gripped her wrist with her free hand, forced herself to walk on slowly and steadily, her reason and her imagination arguing fiercely as she went.

There are more things in heaven and earth than are dreamed of in your philosophy, Joan girl.

And more things in your imagination than ever existed in reality. Do try to think logically and stop acting like an hysterical schoogirl.

She tripped over an unexpected stone, teetered for an instant, and uttered an exclamation of dismay as her hand jerked and the flame of the lamp spluttered and died.

'Oh damn!' The expletive escaped her before she could hold it back.

This was stupid! She had walked quite a long way already. The open gates of the convent grounds couldn't be very far ahead. She walked on again, a faint trail of black smoke punctuating the white mist like an exclamation mark from the lamp in her hand. She tried humming but the sound quavered to nothingness in her throat.

Ahead of her long arrows of light broke through the mist and voices called, seeming to come from all around her.

'Sister! Sister Joan, are you there? Sister!'

'Here! I'm here!' She raised her own voice, standing still as she was caught in the beam of Sister Perpetua's torch.

'Are you all right, Sister?' The infirmarian's bulky frame hove through the white veil.

'Yes. Yes, perfectly all right.'

The habit of maintaining calm wrapped her round as she replied. Self-control was a virtue when it was practised every day. Her own novice mistress had told her that.

'We had a telephone call from Father Malone, asking if you'd arrived home safely. The fog is thick even down in the town and he was worried.'

'The engine died, I think it needs oil. There was nothing to do but walk. I took some pies to Brother Cuthbert but he wasn't there.'

Other members of the community had reached and surrounded them, veils hanging damply round faces bright with relief. Mother Dorothy in the forefront, holding her own torch.

'Apparently Brother Cuthbert decided to walk down into town to meditate in the church for an hour or two,' she said briskly. 'Father Malone met him there and thought he'd better ring us. We came out in twos – not Sister Gabrielle or Sister Mary Concepta, of course. We left them to man the telephone.'

'I left the pies at the schoolhouse,' Sister Joan explained as they walked back towards the gates in a tight little group. 'The van wouldn't start again so I borrowed the lamp and then that ran out of oil too.'

'Like the wise and foolish virgins,' Sister Hilaria said. 'I always felt sorry for the foolish ones myself.'

'In which category Sister Joan can certainly place herself,' Mother Dorothy said. 'It was very careless of you not to check the oil, Sister.'

'I know. I'm very sorry, Reverend Mother.'

'Well, we saved some supper for you,' Sister Perpetua said.

'Thank you, Sister. I'm afraid I've put you to a great deal of trouble.' She spoke meekly, hoping that Mother Dorothy would call her into the parlour so that she could tell her that she had delivered the trowel, but as they came within sight of the main door where Bernadette was framed against the light, anxiously looking out, Mother Dorothy exclaimed.

'Our guests must have come back earlier! You'll be happy to see that Sister Joan is safe and sound. The van broke down.'

'Is Magdalen with you?' Bernadette asked.

'Didn't she come back with you?' Mother Dorothy asked sharply.

Bernadette shook her head, her plaits swinging.

'I lost her in the mist. One minute she was beside me and the next she'd gone. She was nervous about going out to search so I assumed she'd just sneak – slipped back inside. I didn't fancy going on alone so I went back to see if she was around, but Sister Gabrielle says that nobody came back except me.'

'Sister Gabrielle probably didn't see her,' Sister David said, carefully wiping the moisture from her spectacles. 'Shall we go out and look for her or look inside first?'

'We'll look inside first,' Mother Dorothy said firmly. 'She's probably in chapel or in her room. I'll ring Father Malone to let him know that you're back safely, Sister Joan. Your garments look very damp. You'd better come into the kitchen and get warm by the cooker. Will you see to it, Sister Perpetua?'

'Right this minute,' Sister Perpetua said, taking Sister Joan's arm and marching her into the corridor as if she feared she might suddenly bolt. 'I'll whip up some fresh cheese sauce.'

'What I'd really love is a strong cup of tea,' Sister Joan said, entering the kitchen and sinking on to a chair with relief.

'You shall have it at once.' Sister Perpetua bustled to the stove. 'We were very concerned when the mist came down and you weren't back from town. Sister Marie wanted to join us in the search even though her ankle is still hurting. I shall be very glad when things return to normal again.'

'Do you think they ever will, Sister?'

Sister Joan sipped the hot tea and shot a glance towards the other who was busily stirring the contents of a saucepan.

'We've had crises before, Sister, but the spiritual life goes on as does the practical work,' Sister Perpetua said. 'I agree with you though that once fear intrudes into a community it's very hard to root it out again.'

'When I was walking here something went past me in the

mist.' Sister Joan dropped her voice slightly. 'Something big and black, not touching the ground.'

'A bat?' Sister Perpetua drew a small dish of vegetables out of the oven, poured the sauce over, and motioned the younger woman to the table.

'No. It was as big as a human being.'

'Then it probably was a human being,' Sister Perpetua said prosaically. 'Black, you said?'

'A cloak and hood, wide sleeves.'

'Young Brother Cuthbert hasn't taken to levitating, has he?'

'I don't think so.' Sister Joan chuckled at the thought. 'No, this was – someone in a great hurry, whooshing past.'

'On a bike?'

'Sister Perpetua, you're a genius!' Sister Joan put down her spoon and beamed.

'Naturally.' Sister Perpetua winked and was immediately serious again. 'The trouble with you is that you always overlook the obvious. Anyone wearing a long cloak and riding a bike in the darkness or in the fog with no lights visible would look as if they were moving above the ground.'

'But none of us rides a bike.'

'And Brother Cuthbert walks everywhere on those enormous feet. Sister, nuns and friars aren't the only people who wear cloaks.'

'No, but Sylvia Dacre does.'

'Who?'

'A woman called Sylvia Dacre – she's with the new-age travellers. She has a small caravan. I met her briefly.'

'The gadabout nun,' Sister Perpetua said, mildly disapproving. 'Sister, you must stay close to home until Sister Elizabeth's murderer is caught. I do feel that – ah, here comes Bernadette! Would you like a nice cup of tea?'

'No thank you, Sister.' Bernadette, who had just come in, shook her head politely. 'We haven't found Magdalen yet.'

'She must have wandered off by herself.' Sister Perpetua clucked her tongue. 'Have you looked in the chapel?'

'We've looked everywhere in the main building and it's still too foggy to go out again.'

'Someone ought to go. She can't be left roaming around in this fog!' Sister Joan exclaimed. 'Did she have a torch?'

Bernadette nodded.

'We had one between us. When she disappeared she must have switched it off because I couldn't see any light at all. I had to grope my way back to the house.'

'Then she's probably trying to make herself important,' Sister Perpetua said. 'Yes, I'm aware that's an uncharitable comment, but that young woman manages to cause a lot of upset in her meek, quiet way. That doesn't mean that I'm not concerned about her.'

'If you'll excuse me I ought to go and see Reverend Mother.' Sister Joan crossed herself, murmured a hasty grace over her empty plate, and went back towards the parlour.

Mother Dorothy was just replacing the telephone receiver as she knocked and entered.

'*Dominus vobiscum.* What is it, Sister?'

'*Et cum spiritu tuo.* I wondered if anyone had any idea what has happened to Magdalen. Bernadette says she's nowhere to be found.'

'I just rang the police,' Mother Dorothy said crisply.

'But surely we could go and look for her?'

'As we did for you? The mist is even thicker now, and your case was quite different,' her superior frowned. 'You were on your way home and since you were so late it was common sense to assume that the van had broken down and you were either still sitting there or had started walking back along the track. I suspect that Magdalen went off deliberately. That makes a difference.'

'But why would she do that? She's scared of going out alone.'

'I don't know, Sister.' Mother Dorothy frowned again, drummed her fingers on the desk, and added, 'Please keep this to yourself, but someone has been found lying injured on the moor, and I'm very much afraid that it may be Magdalen Cole.'

Eleven

They had been driven to the hospital behind a strange police officer who had glued his eyes to the fog-white windscreen and kept them there. Neither Mother Dorothy nor Sister Joan spoke during the brief journey. Each was occupied with her own thoughts.

Sister Hilaria had been deputed to conduct evening prayers and give the blessing. In less than an hour the grand silence would begin. There would be no opportunity then of discussing events after that until the following morning.

In the town the street lights cut through the mist. The police car picked up speed slightly as it turned into the curving drive of the hospital whose bulk was lit by squares of light from uncurtained windows.

'It was very good of you to come, Sisters.'

Constable Petrie greeted them in casualty, his youthful face heavy with responsibility.

'Constable Petrie, is it not?' Mother Dorothy shook hands briskly. 'What makes you think that the injured woman is Magdalen Cole?'

'She has a letter addressed to Magdalen Cole in her pocket, addressed to the convent,' Constable Petrie informed her. 'Unstamped and not yet opened. Of course I haven't met the lady myself. Detective Sergeant Mill went out of town until tomorrow on personal business so I thought it best to contact the convent directly. If you'll come this way – I'm afraid she's still unconscious.'

The side ward was gleaming white with a shaded pink bulb

to soften the effect. Through the slightly opened window white mist curled. The patient, her head bandaged, a large dressing obscuring her cheek, lay on her back, a nurse seated at the side.

'It's Sylvia Dacre,' Sister Joan said. 'Not Magdalen.'

'You know her, Sister?' Constable Petrie looked at her.

'She came with the new-age travellers. She has a caravan. I met her briefly.'

'Then why would she have a letter addressed to Magdalen Cole?' he puzzled.

'Did she or Magdalen mention having known each other?' Mother Dorothy asked.

Sister Joan shook her head.

'Did Luther see anyone else?' she asked in her turn. 'Anyone who might have attacked Sylvia Dacre?'

'She wasn't attacked, Sister.' The Constable drew them outside into the corridor. 'She crashed her bike in the mist and came off it in a pile of gravel.'

'And she was wearing a long black cape with a hood?'

'Which saved her from even worse injury. How did you know?'

'Luther said he'd seen a bat flying just above the ground. The long cloak would have hidden the wheels.'

'How badly hurt is she?' Mother Dorothy asked.

'Would you like a word with the doctor? It's down here, Reverend Mother.' A tall nursing sister had loomed up, stiffly starched and efficient.

'Wait for me here, Sister.' Mother Dorothy followed the sister to a door marked 'Dr Chasen'.

'Did Sylvia Dacre have nothing else on her apart from the letter?' Sister Joan asked.

'Only the letter. I took charge of it thinking it had been addressed to her, but it looks as if she was writing to Miss Cole herself, doesn't it?'

'Would you like me to take it for her?' Sister Joan's blue eyes were ingenuous.

'That would be very kind of you, Sister. The poor lady will want it delivered, I daresay, but if Miss Cole is missing—'

'She became separated from the others when they came out to look for me. She's a sensible young woman, likely to find herself a shelter and sit tight until morning.'

'In that case—' He dug in his pocket and produced the letter, now slightly crumpled at the edges. 'I'm afraid you'll have to sign for it.'

'Yes, of course.' She signed her name neatly on the page he took from his notebook. 'I'll see that Magdalen gets it as soon as I see her.'

The envelope felt thick and bulky in her deep pocket. She turned as Mother Dorothy emerged from the doctor's office.

'A nasty concussion with a possible hairline fracture of the skull and numerous bruises and abrasions,' she reported. 'Thank God for it might have been worse. Are you ready to go, Sister?'

'Yes, Reverend Mother,' Sister Joan said.

'The car's waiting for you, Sisters.' Constable Petrie led the way out. 'About the young lady who went missing – we are pretty short-handed at the moment, but I'll get some men out on the moor immediately. As you say she may well have found a place where she can shelter until the mist clears.'

'One of the sisters will come down in the morning to see how the patient is doing,' Mother Dorothy told him. 'Oh, but we've no transport! I forgot.'

'The van broke down,' Sister Joan said meekly. 'I left it outside the schoolhouse.'

'I'll have one of the lads see to it and drive it over to you in the morning,' Constable Petrie said.

'That's very kind of you,' Mother Dorothy said, glancing at her watch. 'Would you be good enough to tell the driver who's taking us home now that in five minutes the grand silence begins so we will be unable to thank him properly or bid him good night? The grand silence is only broken in emergencies.'

'Yes, of course, Sisters.' He nodded respectfully, ushering them through the mist to the waiting car.

'When I saw Sylvia Dacre she was on foot,' Sister Joan said

when they were turning into the main road again. 'I suppose she only used a bike when—'

'*In nomine patris et filius et spiritus sanctus.*' Mother Dorothy uttered the blessing as she signed the cross upon the air.

'Amen,' Sister Joan murmured.

The grand silence had begun. There was now no chance to discuss the letter that was in her keeping, no chance to speculate with Mother Dorothy upon the link between Magdalen Cole and Sylvia Dacre. She sat quietly, thoughts circling in her head.

Sister Hilaria stood at the main door with Sister David at her side, both of them peering anxiously. Mother Dorothy shook her head in answer to their questioning looks and turned towards the chapel wing, Sister Joan at her heels. A few minutes' silent prayer would mitigate the loss of the evening devotions.

In the chapel the candles still burned. Sister Joan went to her usual place and knelt, waiting for calm but inside the seething questions jostled for position. The recent sequence of events unrolled in her mind. The two guests had arrived. The new-age travellers had arrived. Sister Marie had been attacked while wearing Magdalen's white headscarf; no, not actually attacked but grabbed from behind. She had injured herself in trying to get away down the steps. Then Sister Elizabeth had been killed, while she slept in the room that Magdalen had been occupying. Magdalen had left the inner door to the chapel wing open and neatly transferred the blame to Bernadette. Sylvia Dacre had sometimes ridden a bike presumably when she wanted to get somewhere quickly. Roses. Roses had turned up in unexpected places. Expensive hothouse roses. Roses for love. People who loved didn't usually kill – but there was nothing usual about these particular circumstances.

Mother Dorothy rose, genuflected, touched her lightly on the shoulder as she went out. The fleeting pat said that it was time to lock up, to extinguish lights, to carry out the normal routine of an acting lay sister.

Sister Joan waited until the door of the chapel had closed with a soft click. She blessed herself, thankful to find that the apprehension filling her was now joined by a feeling of determined energy, and rose. Going up the winding stairs into the library and the storerooms beyond, she was still fitting the recent sequence of events into chronological order in her mind. Sylvia Dacre had been here and gone swiftly up these stairs on the night she herself had come up to the library. That bat-like shape rushing past her in the darkness had been Sylvia Dacre in her distinctive black cape. She hadn't wanted to be seen though there was no reason why a member of the public couldn't have come in from outside to pray in the chapel. And she had left two roses – one in the library, the other dropped on the step. Dropped deliberately or merely because she was in flight?

The upper storey was quiet and still. Sister Joan came down into the chapel again. The outer door was unlocked. She opened it and looked out into the mist, no longer a dense white blanket but swirling into tatters. Overhead stars struggled to be seen.

Extinguishing all the lights save for the sanctuary lamp she locked the inner door and went across to the parlour to check that the windows were securely fastened. Then she went upstairs to make similar checks on the dining-room and recreation rooms, trod softly down the upper corridor past the closed doors of the quiet cells, turned the main light to its dimmest point and came downstairs again.

The kitchen was still warm, the back door bolted, shutters drawn down at the window. Alice's empty basket struck a sad note. She would be glad when the dog was back from her training course. Through the wall she could hear Sister Mary Concepta's gentle snores. It had been a long day for the old ladies. Even Sister Gabrielle must be asleep. She moved to the door of the lay cell where Sister Elizabeth had slept and opened it. The bed had been stripped. Faintly pencilled circles indicated where finger prints had been found, but she suspected they would all prove to be innocent. This killer was far too cautious to leave prints.

She was still wearing her outdoor cloak. She went into the kitchen and took a torch out of one of the drawers. It was time for her to deliver the letter, and she had a shrewd suspicion where the intended recipient would be.

Outside she switched on the torch to half power and held it behind her palm lest a stray gleam be seen by any wakeful soul within the main house. The grounds all about her seemed to have entered into the grand silence. Trees and bushes stood mute and dripping and the ground underfoot yielded with no more than the faintest of squishing sounds.

She went through the gate into the burial plot and stood for a moment by the flower-strewn mound of earth. Sister Elizabeth had been a good girl. A good, quiet girl who would have been a valued member of the community. She should have been allowed to live out her peaceful, unremarkable existence. Whoever had killed her was wicked.

'Judge not that ye be not judged' had been one of the maxims that had been drilled into her by her first novice mistress. There is never any good reason for murder, her own mind argued.

She had reached the steps leading to the tennis courts and she risked turning the torch on full and sweeping it in a wide arc over the hanging nets, the grass-grown courts. It was silent and deserted, mist beginning almost imperceptibly to lift, to billow in great curtains before her. The air smelt of damp earth.

She walked steadily down the steps and across the courts. The postulancy was in darkness. She opened the low wicker gate and went to the front door, pushing it and finding it, as she had expected, unlocked.

Inside the narrow lobby-like hall was empty, her own shadow leaping against the whitewashed walls as she swung the beam of light around. She shone the torch up the stairs and called softly,

'Magdalen? Magdalen, it's safe to come down now.'

From the top of the stairs a shadow uncurled itself from the

deeper shadows. Magdalen came slowly down the stairs, her
coat huddled around her. She looked tired and strained, her
clear grey eyes dark circled.

'How did you guess that I was here?' she asked.

'I didn't think you'd leave the enclosure and it occurred to
me that you might have taken the spare key to the postulancy
when you were with Bernadette. This would be a safe place to
hide.'

'I had to hide somewhere,' Magdalen said. 'We went out to
look for you, Sister. I really didn't want to go but when
Bernadette volunteered then I didn't like to refuse. It was
scary out there with the mist so thick and even our footsteps
muffled. I let go of Bernadette's arm and switched off the
torch and melted away. It took her a minute before she
realized she was by herself, but I heard her voice calling and
one of the other sisters answering so I knew she'd be all right.'

'And you made your way to the postulancy?'

'I hid in the shrubbery for a bit but I didn't feel safe there,
and then I remembered that I had the key so I came here and
let myself in.'

'And left the door unlocked?' Sister Joan said mildly.

'I must've forgotten it,' Magdalen said. 'Sister, there's a
murderer about and yet you sound so calm! Doesn't anyone
care?'

'Why did you leave the door unlocked? Were you waiting
for Sylvia Dacre?' Sister Joan persisted.

'Who?'

'Sylvia Dacre had an accident earlier this evening while she
was riding her bike over the moor.'

'Then I don't have anything to fear any longer!'
Magdalen's voice vibrated with relief.

'You were afraid of Sylvia Dacre?'

'Oh yes.' Magdalen paused and sat down on the stairs,
leaning her chin on her hand. 'She has been pestering me for
ages, you know. A dreadful, twisted kind of devotion. That's
wrong, isn't it, Sister? Against the law of God!'

'The Old Testament does seem to be clear on that point,'

Sister Joan said.

'Wicked, twisted desires,' Magdalen said. 'I thought that I'd be safe here, that she wouldn't find me, but I was wrong. She's still hunting, Sister. Was it a bad accident she had? Is she going to die?'

'I don't think so. She was coming here with a letter for you but for some reason she didn't deliver it.'

'A letter? Where is it now?' Magdalen's voice had sharpened.

'I said that I would deliver it. I think it contains a rose.'

Sister Joan took out the thick envelope and handed it over.

'A rose?' Magdalen's fingers tore open the envelope.

'Why roses?' Sister Joan asked. 'There were other roses left, ones that you didn't find. Why roses?'

'She owns a small florist's shop, very exclusive.' Magdalen took out the flower, held it between the tips of her fingers, and dropped it on to the floor.

'If she means to harm you why should she try to send you warning?' Sister Joan asked.

'How should I know?' Magdalen shrugged impatiently.

'When Sister Marie was grabbed near the tennis courts – Sylvia Dacre couldn't have mistaken her for you surely, even if she was wearing your scarf?'

'She wanted to attract Sister Marie's attention, to ask her if I was here.'

'Then she wasn't sure?'

'Probably not, since I tried to cover my tracks,' Magdalen said. 'She probably went to the priest and charmed him into telling her where I'd gone. Not his fault. He assumed we were just friends.'

"You were more than friends?'

'I don't know what you mean.' Magdalen's expression was sulky. 'She pestered me, that's all. Why are you asking me all these questions?'

'Because it doesn't make sense,' Sister Joan said. 'You say this woman was after you, meaning to do you harm because you wouldn't give in to her advances?'

'Exactly! She was pestering me. It was exactly like that.'

'But you just said that your parish priest assumed you were friends. Did Sylvia Dacre have any reason to suppose that you might not mind her affections?'

'People can get tired of people,' Magdalen muttered. 'We'd been together for five years. That's a long time. I was sick of her, sick of being adored and cossetted and wrapped up in loving care. I wanted to get away and she wouldn't let me go. She said that she'd always follow me, always be devoted to me – and she's old! She's nearly fifty and I wanted to be free of her.'

'You lived together then?'

'We weren't legally bound!' Magdalen had half-risen, anger in her face. 'I told her to find a new partner but she kept saying she was devoted to me. Then I decided to enter a convent.'

'I'm sorry to disappoint you,' Sister Joan said dryly, 'but your way of loving is most strongly discouraged in the religious orders.'

'Everybody has a chink in their armour,' Magdalen said.

'Did Sister Elizabeth?'

'She was so quiet and gentle.' Magdalen's eyes clouded briefly. 'I thought that she had a loving heart. When we were going round the postulancy I lagged behind a little and put my hand over hers, just to test the waters, so to speak. She drew away and gave me such a cold look, a shrinking look. You could tell she had a dirty mind. Certainly she wasn't fit to be a nun.'

'She was innocent but not ignorant,' Sister Joan said.

'She would have told somebody,' Magdalen said. 'I knew she would have felt obliged to tell someone, to make more of it than it was.'

'So you killed her?'

Her heart was hammering again.

'It was necessary,' Magdalen said, with what seemed like

genuine regret. 'I couldn't have them deny me entry, you see. She didn't suffer. Honestly, she never even woke up.'

'And then you opened the inner door leading to the chapel wing hoping that an intruder from outside would be blamed.'

'I did think of admitting that I'd done that by accident,' Magdalen said. 'I did say that I'd been into the chapel. I was afraid that one of the old nuns in the infirmary might have been awake when I left the room, so it would have looked suspicious if I hadn't said anything at all. And then afterwards it occurred to me that I might get sent away anyway for being so careless so I blamed Bernadette. She isn't a very suitable candidate either. Did you know she was engaged and broke off her engagement when she came here?'

'And Sylvia Dacre? What of her?'

'She was coming through the mist to find me,' Magdalen said tensely. 'It was the most dreadful situation, Sister. Knowing she was coming and not being able to do a thing about it. I slipped out just after supper while they were deciding whether or not to go in search of you and I saw her, looming up like a great bat. I was in the driveway and I told her what I'd done. I told her that she'd be blamed for Sister Elizabeth's death. I told her there were clues. She wheeled the bike around and set off like a – a bat out of hell! That's rather a good simile, isn't it, Sister? A bat out of hell! She was frightened, you see. So frightened that she forgot to deliver the rose. They were always the token of love between us in the old days. She was always stupid and sentimental.'

'She's going to testify against you,' Sister Joan said. She spoke gently, holding herself tensely in the light cast by the torch.

'No she won't.' Magdalen's voice was soft. 'She's devoted to me, Sister. She won't repeat what I said to her. And you won't either.'

'Won't I?' Sister Joan asked.

'This is the grand silence. If you confess you broke the grand silence they might send you away from here. That's a very strict rule, isn't it? Anyway, you do like me, don't you? Don't you? You're a pretty woman, Sister. A very pretty woman. Do you never think of that in the night when you lie in your cell? Do you, Sister?'

Magdalen was reaching for her, their two shadows leaning together in the confined space.

The door was behind her. She took a step backwards and wrenched it open, turning to flee, feeling a blow at her shoulder as she fled, hearing the clang as the torch clattered to the floor.

She was running through the jagged curtains of mist, making her way blindly across the tennis courts, hearing Magdalen's voice too close behind.

'I won't need a trowel now, Sister! I've got the torch. I've got a heavy torch! We can be friends you and I! I don't have to do this! Come back, Sister dear!'

She had reached the steps and stood for a moment, panting, sweat mingling with the coldness of the mist. Behind her Magdalen ran forward, switching on the torch, its long beam sweeping round in an arc.

Sister Joan ran up the steps and stumbled along the narrow path with its high borders of shrubbery. There was another sound now – the rustling of wet leaves on their evergreen stems, the sound of a voice hissing.

'Left, turn left.'

At the last moment, as the torch descended, she flung herself sideways and landed in a patch of bramble on her hands and knees. There was scuffling close by, a voice shouting in impotent fury, 'It wasn't me! She is not running away from me!'

A stronger light shone on her face. An arm reached down and hauled her to her feet.

'You can relax, Sister,' Detective Sergeant Mill said. 'We have Magdalen Cole in custody.'

'How did you get here?' She leaned limply against the trunk of a nearby tree, pulling her cloak about her, shivering.

'Let's get you inside first. Come along.'

His hand was beneath her elbow and she went unresistingly, surprised at the shakiness of her legs. Ahead of them a violently protesting Magdalen was being thrust into a police car by two uniformed constables.

There were lights in the kitchen with Mother Dorothy astonishingly brewing tea and Sister Perpetua peering anxiously out of the back door.

'You need not trouble to tell me that you've broken the grand silence,' Mother Dorothy said, pouring tea and nodding towards a chair. 'I am of the opinion that this evening constitutes a legitimate emergency. You are not hurt?'

'No, Reverend Mother. A few scratches, nothing more – but how on earth—'

'I called in at the station on my way home and saw Constable Petrie who told me about Sylvia Dacre's accident,' Detective Sergeant Mill said, accepting a cup of tea with a murmur of thanks. 'He said you and the reverend mother here had just started back from the hospital and that he'd given you the letter for Magdalen Cole found on Sylvia Dacre. I picked up a couple of lads and drove here after you. I'd made several phone calls this afternoon. Magdalen Cole's parish priest told me that she and Sylvia Dacre shared a flat over the florist's shop. He regarded them as good friends but Sylvia Dacre became so upset when she learned that her friend intended to become a nun that her reaction worried him. Anyway when I arrived you had just slipped out, leaving the kitchen door unlocked. Mother Dorothy was still awake and on the verge of setting out to look for you with Sister Perpetua here.'

'But how—?' Sister Joan looked at them both.

'We know you far too well to believe that you'd go tamely to bed when one of us was missing,' Sister Perpetua said.

'We requested the sisters to stay here and followed you,' Detective Sergeant Mill said. 'Unfortunately we were a good distance behind. By the time we reached the shrubbery you were fleeing for your life across the tennis court. We'd no option but to lie low and grab her as she reached the top of the steps.'

'Then you didn't know that she had killed Sister Elizabeth?'

'Not really. I mean that at that stage we had no proof. It was only a hunch on my part. Wherever we turned in the case Magdalen Cole kept popping up, as the really intended victim according to the sequence of events, but when the intended victim keeps escaping then it's time to turn things around, look at them in another way.'

'Meaning that nobody wanted to hurt Magdalen at all?' Sister Joan said, gulping tea.

'If you're trying to sneak up on someone and kill them then you don't drop roses around the district to hint at your presence,' he said. 'And her asking you to get her a rape alarm – if she was truly frightened then surely she'd have bought one before she came.'

'Did you know that Magdalen – I suppose she is the person responsible?' Mother Dorothy glanced at the detective.

'Seems clear enough from what she was yelling,' he said, distaste in his face. 'She was sick of her partner, Sylvia Dacre, and thought she might find a younger friend within the convent.'

'Detective Sergeant Mill, we don't go in for that kind of thing here!' Sister Perpetua said, outraged.

'She made a tentative advance to Sister Elizabeth,' Sister Joan said. 'When Sister Elizabeth drew away, looking horrified, she was afraid that she might say something about the incident so she killed her, left the inner door open, and hoped that if we did link her with Sylvia Dacre then we'd assume that Sylvia Dacre had sneaked in to attack her and mistaken Sister Elizabeth for Magdalen since they'd just changed cells.'

'That wouldn't have held water,' Detective Sergeant Mill said. 'Since Sylvia Dacre didn't know who was sleeping where why should she have made straight for the cell where Sister Elizabeth was?'

'She still might have had some explaining to do.' He set down the cup and rose from the chair where he had been sitting. 'We'll be talking to Miss Dacre in the morning when she's fully conscious, but I reckon that she followed Magdalen here hoping to persuade her to go back with her. Hence the roses, her attempt to speak to Sister Marie – yes, I'm fairly certain that she was the intruder in the grounds. Again not a case of mistaken identity at all, but it suited Magdalen Cole to pretend to believe that it was. She could have had Sylvia Dacre picked up for harassment, attempted abduction, whatever.'

'And in the end she could have accused her of murder,' Sister Joan said.

'Let us hope that she wouldn't have allowed it to go so far,' Mother Dorothy said.

'I'd better get down to the station and contact the hospital again,' Detective Sergeant Mill said. 'My apologies for disturbing the grand silence. Goodnight.'

'I'll see you to the door.' Mother Dorothy went with him into the corridor.

'I knew there was something peculiar about her,' Sister Perpetua said. 'Couldn't put my finger exactly on what it was. Well, I suppose the only good thing to be said is that she'd left her partner.'

'Hoping to find someone younger among the community,' Sister Joan said bleakly.

'And poor Sister Elizabeth was the one chosen.' Sister Perpetua shook her head. 'Love has some twisted paths leading to the heart of it! Sister, go to bed now. At least we can keep silence from now until morning. Come morning I've no doubt that Mother Dorothy will be wanting a few words with you.'

'I know she will,' Sister Joan said gloomily, and went tiredly into the lay cell, closing the door softly, moving to shutter the window.

Outside the mist was blowing spirals round the corners of

the stable. As it lifted from the ground like billows of dense white lawn the gleaming wet cobbles were revealed, shining faintly under the emerging moon.

She leaned her forehead briefly against the smudged pane and sighed. Love had indeed many twisted paths. Somewhere at the place where they all met was the truth of it but it was hidden like the cobbles beneath the mist. Suddenly she wanted to cry.

Sister Teresa had made a beautiful bride. Her velvet dress with its heart-shaped cap from which a short veil floated, the delicate sheaf of flowers, had given her height and dignity. Her short brown curls had clustered around her face and her smile had been joyful. Spring with all its promise of eternal life was surely the best time to make one's final profession, Sister Joan mused, rising as Sister Teresa, now lay sister in the Order of the Daughters of Compassion, re-entered the chapel in the grey habit and short white veil she would wear from now on. The velvet dress would be given to a bride as a gift from the convent but Sister Teresa would have her photographs to remind her. Those and the well-wishers who had come to see her make her final vows.

The ceremony was ending. Sandwiches, wine and coffee had been set out in the dining-room for everybody who cared to partake of them. As Brother Cuthbert's lute caressed the air the procession formed, Sister Teresa blushing and beaming in her new habit as she came down the short aisle to receive congratulations.

'Bernadette!' Coming out into the main hall, Sister Joan spotted the swinging plait and merry dark eyes. 'How kind of you to come!'

'Didn't Mother Dorothy tell you?' Bernadette shook hands warmly. 'I've been accepted for the novitiate. I start next month.'

'That's marvellous!' Sister Joan's smile widened with pleasure. 'I'm really pleased you're joining us though it'll be a couple of years before we can chat together freely again.'

'I daresay we'll find opportunity,' Bernadette said with a twinkle. 'I'll rattle around a bit in the postulancy though. Maybe more will come.'

'Where vocations are concerned it's quality not quantity,' Sister Joan quoted. 'You're sure about this?'

'Very sure. I was engaged, you know,' Bernadette said, lowering her voice. 'He was such a nice person and I was very fond of him but being with him wasn't enough.'

'Was his name Julian?'

'Yes, it is! How did you guess?' Bernadette looked at her in surprise.

'I'm psychic,' Sister Joan said bluntly, thinking of the two young men who had travelled down to the area. Had they hoped to see Bernadette and persuade her out of her resolution? And had they changed their minds and gone away, leaving the girl to live her life as she wished? Then young Julian must have loved greatly. Sister Joan reminded herself to include young Julian in her prayers and turned to Bernadette again.

'Go upstairs and have some refreshments. I have a task to perform before I join you,' she said.

Sister Teresa's bouquet lay on the bench by the chapel door. She picked up the sheaf of lilies and tiny, creamy rosebuds and carried them outside into the spring sunshine. Sister Elizabeth's grave had a coating of short grass starred with daisies. She laid the flowers on it as Sister Teresa had requested and stood with bent head.

'Sister Joan?'

'Detective Sergeant Mill, how good to see you! Did you come to the ceremony?' Turning at the sound of his voice she smiled at him.

'I didn't come to the ceremony. Not much in my line.' He spoke almost curtly.

'You'd look silly in a white dress,' she said mildly.

'Indeed I would! I wish Sister Teresa all the best, however. I came over to tell you that I've had a letter from Sylvia Dacre.'

'How is she?'

'Trying to rebuild her life. She really loved that nasty little piece of work.'

'Yes, I know,' Sister Joan said soberly. 'What happens now?'

'Magdalen Cole is trying to convince everybody she's insane. It won't wash, you know. She'll get a hefty prison term, the longer the better as far as I'm concerned. You'll have to give evidence but we'll make it as low key as possible. That won't be for months yet. Sylvia Dacre didn't realize how dangerous Magdalen was until she got on her bike and came up to deliver that letter – well, rose, to the young woman. Magdalen told her that she'd killed Sister Elizabeth and Miss Dacre rode off in a blind panic. That must have been hard for her. Finding out that the person you've been wooing back with roses is a killer. I've a lot of sympathy for her.'

'So have I,' Sister Joan said. 'Poor lady.'

'So!' He stood back a little, frowning slightly, then said abruptly, 'What I really came to say was that my wife and I – well, we've decided to try to have another go at the marriage for the sake of the boys. I haven't very high hopes but I'll be doing my best. I wanted you to know.'

'I'm truly delighted!' Sister Joan's face lit up. 'Oh, I know you're both doing the right thing. I do wish you both every happiness.'

'Happiness? Well, maybe there's a spark still to blow on. I'm grateful for your friendship, Sister.'

'And I for yours, Detective Sergeant Mill. If you'll excuse me now I have to get back to the celebrations. My best wishes.'

She had taken a couple of steps as he bent to the flowers and broke off a short-stemmed white rosebud.

'Flowers for a nun?' she said lightly as he handed her the bloom.

'A rosebud for a pretty woman,' he said. 'It's a shame it

won't ever grow into a full petalled rose.'

'I'll put it on the altar,' Sister Joan said. 'It'll bloom there. God bless.' And turning again, her step light, she went swiftly towards the chapel.